Keeley's Fight

Keeley's Fight
The Protectors Series Book 1
Copyright © 2015 Krystal Fahl
Print Edition

If you or someone you know may be in a domestic violence situation please get help. No matter who you are, you are worth it. Keep on Fighting. You can find more information on domestic violence at The National Domestic Violence Hotline website here:
www.thehotline.org

Cover design by Tammie Smith.
www.facebook.com/pages/Author-Tammie-Smith/510347269117830

Editing done by KA Matthews from K&J Book Promotions.
www.facebook.com/pages/KJ-Book-Promotions/1598454617069604

Blurb

Heartache and betrayal are two things Keeley Stone is very familiar with. Born into a life she never wanted, betrayed by her own parents, she never saw a way out. Until one day, two men who know nothing of her or her life step up and protect her when she's in need of a savior.

Loyalty and respect are not just something earned for brothers Nathaniel and Tyler Maxwell, but a code they live by. A chance encounter with a gorgeous young woman has left them enthralled with her.

Can they convince her they're worth fighting for? Or will she let demons of her past control her future?

Note: This is a stand-alone HEA M/F/M contemporary romance novel. There is no touching for titillation between brothers.

Acknowledgements

Thank you to my betas for all your feedback, and not telling me it's a complete mess! Jeannie G, Jamie S, Yolanda B, Danielle M, Tracey S, Ashley R, Mindy M, Francesca A, and Tamra S, love you all to the moon and back! Your notes and messages kept me going and helped make Keeley as awesome as she is!

My editor KA Matthews for taking a chance on a newbie like me, it was such a joy to work with you! Tammie Smith for creating my cover, it's stunning and perfect and I love it and you!

Sara Bartlett and Joanna Blake for always asking me how it's going and encouraging me to continue, and making me laugh every time we talk, I love you ladies!!

Winter Travers, Annelise Reynolds, Veronica Garcia, Lana Robbins Hill and Lauren Martin, you're enthusiasm to read Keeley has left me breathless at times and I can't thank you enough for all your support!!!

Jordan Marie for all your recommendations and advice and everything in between! Everything you've done for me first as a reader, then as a blogger, and now as an author, I will never be able to repay you, and I sincerely hope you know how amazing you are as not just an author (Cause you do kickass!) But also as a person, I couldn't ask for a better friend!! Love your face chick!

Honey Palomino, Autumn Jones Lake, Leslie Wilder, CM Steele, Sapphire Knight and Kaylee Song, for encouraging me even when I hesitated and telling me how excited you all are to read it!! Much love ladies!!

Sherri, my fellow Canuck, thank you for helping with well all the legal crap, it helped immensely!

Again to Jamie Sexton if it weren't for you forcing me to send you what I had and telling me it was worth finishing I probably never would have done it, so I thank you from the very bottom of my heart!!!!

My awesome street team KL's Fighters, you girls rock it!!!

Some amazing blogs as well, Sisi's Book Whore's, Just One More Page, Abbey's One-Click Book Blog, One Last Page Book Blog, K&J Promotions, Life With 2 Boys and all the fans from my own blog, Not Another Damn Blog-Blog, you all mean the world to me!! Thank you for everything!!!

Finally to everyone who has taken a chance on me and buying this book, it means the world to me and I hope you enjoy Keeley, Nate and Ty as much as I did writing them!

Dedication

To my husband who put up with endless hours of me writing and editing and basically ignoring everyone and everything. My Mom and Grandma for their unwavering support. Savannah, my girl, for telling me "that's so cool, my mom's an author" And my boys, for keeping the house loud making it easier to write :) I love you all more than you'll know!!

KEELEY'S FIGHT

The Protectors Series
Book 1

By KL Donn

Prologue

AT TWELVE YEARS old, Keeley Stone knew three things about life. First, her family wasn't normal. The things her parents did and said to her were not right. The beatings, the name calling, and the lies were all she knew. She didn't know love or even friendship. When she was younger, she thought all moms and dads did these things to their kids. She was wrong. Second, her parents were monsters. They could act like normal people when they wanted, but she knew the truth behind the lies. Her mom cleaned the house and didn't drink for a whole day. She made cookies and hung up some of Keeley's most recent art work on the fridge that she thought they had thrown out when she showed them. Her dad was being nice, telling her how pretty she looked and how smart she was. Neither of them had been drinking all day. She was so happy, she thought things were finally going to get better. That they were going to stop with the drinking and beatings. How wrong she was.

Today was the day that would shape the rest of her life. After dinner, a meal her mom actually cooked, a nice older woman came to the house to speak to her parents and then her.

"So the school tells me that you plan on homeschooling Keeley now Mrs. Stone, is that correct?"

"Oh yes, there are just too many bad influences in that school for such an impressionable young lady like Keeley. We feel like she would excel more at home than there," her mom said, and all Keeley could do was stare at her with her mouth wide open, in complete shock. What was she talking about? There was nothing wrong with her school. That was her salvation, the only time she could really cope with her life.

"Alright, and you have all the resources you need then? May I see them, please?" The lady, Carol she thought she said her name was, asked her mom and dad.

"Of course, I'll be right back with them. Keeley, could you come and give me a hand?" Her dad asked her, making it out like a question for the social worker's benefit.

Following her dad into her parents' bedroom, Keeley still had no idea what was going on, but she soon found out. "Not one fucking word little girl, you hear me? You play along with everything we say, or the beating I've been itching to give you all day, just to wipe that stupid look off your face, will be so much worse tonight, ya hear?" He whisper-yelled to her.

Nodding her head vigorously, she grabbed the stuff her father told her to and walked out to the living room so that Carol could review them. "Well, everything looks in order here. I just have a few questions for Keeley before

I go, if you don't mind?"

Nodding their heads before leaving the room, Keeley caught the warning look in her father's eyes before turning her attention to Carol. Trying not to fidget, she waited for the questions to come.

"How do you like school Keeley, did you find it difficult to concentrate there?"

"Not really, no. I like it well enough I guess."

"How do you feel about being homeschooled by your parents?"

Remembering her father's warning, she thought about her answer before speaking yet another lie to someone who could probably help her, but she was too afraid. "Well, I was shocked at first, but Mom made it sound like so much fun that I'm looking forward to it now. Plus, I'll get to spend more time with Mom and Dad," she replied to Carol with her fake smile firmly in place, and her heart breaking just a little bit more with each false word she spoke.

"What about seeing your friends? Do you think this will affect your relationships with any of them?"

"Oh... Ummmm... you see, I don't really have any friends, so I guess it won't matter." She had to force the truth of those words out and look down, so that Carol wouldn't see the tears in her eyes. It wasn't that she didn't want friends, she just wasn't allowed to have them. Plus, she got sick of always having to lie about the bruising and broken bones, and whatever else was wrong with her.

Shocked, Carol inquired, "None, at all?" Shaking her

head no, Carol moved on to the next few questions, which Keeley just lied her way through so that no one would ever know the truth about what happened behind the walls of her house.

After speaking with her parents a few more minutes, Carol finally left and Keeley tried to slink off to her room in the hopes that her dad would forget about the beating he promised her.

Luck wasn't with her. It never was lately.

"You little bitch! Where do you think you're going?" Her father yelled while grabbing a handful of her hair in one hand and holding a bottle of whiskey in his other. Taking a swig of the foul-smelling stuff, he lifted her up by the hair and smashed her face off the wall. She bit her lip so she wouldn't cry out, because that only enraged him more for some reason. She kept her mouth shut and didn't answer him. Closing her eyes and waiting for this to end was her only choice.

The third thing she knew, she had to get out or she was dead.

Chapter 1

ANOTHER DAY GONE, another wasted day. It was all Keeley Stone could think about. She felt like she was wasting her life away. She worked to give her father, Mack Stone, all her money so he could drink it away. She had been working since she was fourteen years old. First, it was part-time at different restaurants or cleaning houses in the neighborhood. Then a year later her parents gave up the ruse completely, forcing her to drop out of high school altogether. That's all her homeschooling had been, a scheme to keep the state off their back about what she was doing at home. It was a way for her parents to keep her there. She was just labor to them, a money maker, only doing the minimum required schoolwork to keep social services from investigating. She was a way to support their drinking habit, until her mother was killed in a car accident almost a year ago. Now, without the little income her mother did have from the gas station she worked at, it was up to Keeley to pay all the bills and support her father's drinking habit. Since her mother's death, she has been able to at least pay the rent and get a paltry amount of food so she wasn't solely relying on handouts from her greasy, dirty, no-good boss. He was always trying to cop a feel. And even though the other waitresses had told him to back off and leave her alone, he still didn't. She had been working at Fred and Eleanor's Diner for just over two years now, and Fred had been hitting on her ever since. Eleanor, of course, blamed Keeley for it and made her life miserable every time they worked the same shift.

Lately, the abuse had gotten worse though. Fred cornered her in the big freezer one day, about a month ago, and even though you could clearly see her struggling and saying no, Eleanor walked in and blamed her. Again. Eleanor had slapped her across the face and told her this wasn't a house for whores. Since then, Keeley has been avoiding the both of them like the plague. She always tried to make sure someone was with her when she had to go in the back, and it had mostly been working, too. But she knew her time was limited and she'd run into one, or worse, both of them, by herself sooner or later. And that's when the shit was really going to hit the fan.

It's time, she thought. Time to leave this city. Leave this life. Leave her father behind for good. Keeley was going to work just until her next payday, and then just leave for good and never look back. She didn't have high hopes for herself, after all; she had to drop out of high school to start working full-time to support the household bills, as well as her parents. All she wanted was some peace and something stable, without fear of being hit or yelled at for no reason.

She always tried to work the night shift. The tips sucked because it wasn't as busy, but at least she could avoid not only Fred and Eleanor but her father as well, since that's when he was drinking and slept the day away mostly. Something was about to happen though, she could just feel it. And it wasn't going to be good.

As she walked into the diner, two things happened simultaneously. One, Keeley saw two of the most amazingly handsome men she had ever seen in her life. They were both tall, even sitting down. They easily had to be about six feet four inches tall and very rugged looking. Both had short cropped military-style haircuts, dirty blonde in color if she had to guess. One had deep brown eyes and the other had hazel, and they were freaking huge. Built like linebackers. They awoke something in her she had never felt before. She was confused by it, had never felt that tightness in her chest or arousal low in her abdomen.

Then the second thing happened, this one much worse. Eleanor came out of the back yelling in that screechy voice of hers, "Fred you no good, cheating, fucking piece of shit man!! How could you sleep with that dirty little slut?!" Fred, like usual, just ignored her, which pissed her off even more and that anger came directed at Keeley, since she was just walking in.

"Well, if it isn't the little slut?" Eleanor spits out.

"Look Eleanor, I'm sorry Fred's being such a jerk, but I swear it hasn't been, nor will it ever be with me," she tried to reason with her.

SLAP!! She heard it before she felt it.

"Shut the fuck up, bitch! The only reason you're still around is because if you weren't, his filthy paws would be all over me." Eleanor just carried on while Keeley bent her head in shame, and so no one could see the silent tears tracking down her cheeks as she practically ran to the employee restroom, while Eleanor continued her rant.

As she stood in the dingy looking bathroom, with its outdated and cracked tiled flooring and peeling painted walls, all she could think was—*Is this seriously my life?*

There was a bruise already forming on her cheekbone, and right below her right eye. "Gonna be a good shiner by tomorrow," she whispered to herself, "but not the worst, either." Sighing, she walked out of the bathroom to start her shift and nearly collided with Fred.

"What's taking you so long in there, girl? Tables are waiting on you. Get to it," he said angrily then walked away.

Talking to herself she said, *I can do this, just two more weeks.* She walked out to the main room with her head held high and her shoulders straight.

Chapter 2

NATHANIEL AND TYLER Maxwell sat there in stunned silence, as they watched the gorgeous young woman run to the back room after getting slapped so hard it sounded like the crack of a whip. This was the place their mother, Amber, had told them had the best pancakes in all of Austin, Texas. Hard to believe, when the owners abuse their employees.

"Do you think she's ok, Nate?" Ty asked.

"I dunno man, that was fucking harsh, but Ma swears this place is worth the ignorance of the owners," Nate replied back. The cracked vinyl seats and the dingy black and white checkered floors told a whole other story.

But that girl, she was something to look at, and if Nate was a betting man he'd say his little brother was thinking the same thing. She was what was so great about this place, since their mother told them what time of day to come in, and it was approaching one a.m. now. Not exactly pancake time to him.

"You think she's why Ma keeps boasting about this place, don't you?" Ty said, echoing his thoughts.

"Yeah, I really do. Here she comes."

As she started walking closer to them, Nate really got a good look at her and she was breathtaking. Hair the color of a raven, and the bluest eyes he'd ever seen; they were almost crystal. A cute little button nose, with the fullest pink lips that were made for kissing. The only flaw was the bruise forming on her cheek from that slap, and the tear tracks down her cheeks that showed it had hurt as much as he suspected it did.

Nate looked over at Ty to see him completely riveted to the young woman. He had to nudge his leg to get him to shut his mouth, so he didn't start drooling. "But dude…," he said.

"Ya man, this is the reason," Nate whispered back.

"Good evening gentlemen, or rather morning I guess, can I get you some coffee?" She asked them in an almost whisper that Nate really had to strain to hear.

"Sure thing, darlin'," Ty responded for them both. As she turned and walked away, Nate couldn't help but feel a little angry. That young woman was suffering from more than just a slap to the face. She had a dejected look to her. Face down, shoulders slumped forward, and those gorgeous eyes looked dead, when they should have the sparkle of life in them. He wondered about her and what gave her that look.

"She doesn't look good, Nate. And I mean more than just that bruise. She's too thin, despite what the baggy clothes might suggest. She seems a little too pale as well. But fuck is she ever gorgeous. Did you get a look at those eyes, man? Never seen anything like it, and those luscious red lips. Damn." He agreed with Ty's assessment of her, but he swore he heard his brother sigh at that last part, too.

"How old do you think she is, Ty?" Nate asked him.

"She can't be a day over twenty-two," he replied just before she brought their coffee over.

"Here you go. Have you decided what you'd like, or do you need more time?" She could clearly see the menus closed, so Nate didn't even think she was really paying attention, more like just going through the motions.

"Just the coffee for now, thanks," Nate told her. "Why don't you sit down and join us for a few minutes?" He asked impulsively, surprising not only himself but Ty as well. Knowing that he was moving too fast, but couldn't seem to help himself.

"Oh, uh, thank you, but I really can't. Now if you'll excuse me, I need to get back to work," she said.

Ty looked around noting there was no one else in the diner, so he grabbed her hand and turned up the charm he was known for. "Come on darlin', there ain't no one else in here and you look like you could use a cup." He smiled at her but she still hadn't looked up yet, she just stood there frozen. So Ty gave a little tug, and she fell onto the bench seat next to him. When she looked up and made eye contact for the first time with Nate that was when he froze. He had never seen such fear in anyone's eyes before.

"It's alright miss, we just wanted some company. Ty there gets a little annoying sometimes, if ya know what I mean?" Nate tried a soft smile, hoping to calm her down. She looked down and stared at her hands, like they were the most fascinating things in the world. "How about telling us your name?" Nate held his breath as she looked at Ty first and then him. Some of the fear was gone, but you could still see it lurking in the back of her eyes.

"I..I..It's Keeley," she stammered out, with her voice getting a little stronger near the end, and he couldn't help but smile as she spoke.

"Well, I'm Tyler Maxwell and this here is my big brother Nathaniel. It's a pleasure to meet you, Keeley." Ty smiled all dimples just for her, and held out his hand hoping she'd shake it. Nate held his breath, as she almost held in the wince when Ty produced his hand for her to shake. If he hadn't been watching for that exact reaction, he would have missed it for sure. But now he knew. A man had hit her. It pissed him the hell off but he kept all that anger to himself, so as not to scare her with it.

TY FELT SUCH anger at whoever had hurt this gorgeous, fragile young woman, but then he felt incredibly proud as she took his hand to shake. The minute Keeley took his hand he felt it. This zing that went straight up his arm and embedded this tiny woman into his heart. He just knew she was the reason their Ma had sent them here. She was it. Theirs, forever. He could feel it, and he knew Nate would too. She pulled her hand away quickly and held it to her chest, as if she had felt it as well.

Nate gave him a funny look like he had squeezed her too hard or something, so Ty just nodded his head for him to shake her hand. He stuck his out waiting for her to shake, and when she did both their eyes widened. A huge smile spread across Nate's face, and Keeley pulled her hand back again and said, "What'd you do, rub a carpet before coming in here?" They both barked out a laugh at what she said, and she looked so startled, like she hadn't meant to say that out loud. But the look on her face was comical, until a deep blush crept up her neck and hit her face, turning her a nice shade of red that had them smiling at her unwarranted embarrassment.

Ty was still watching her as Nate started to speak, "How old are you, Keeley?" The question startling her again.

"I'll be twenty on April first," she answered. Ty and Nate couldn't be more shocked at her response, for two reasons. One being that she was younger than they originally thought, and two was that she hadn't realized today was that day.

"That's today, darlin'," Ty said.

"Oh," she said as she looked down at her watch. "I guess it is."

They both just sat there utterly stunned that this gorgeous, now twenty-year-old woman wasn't more excited about it being her birthday. "Do you have any plans to go celebrate with your folks or some friends?" Nate questioned her.

She just looked at Nate like that was utterly ridiculous

before replying, "No, my mom's dead and my dad's busy," was all she said before getting up and walking away.

Chapter 3

KEELEY FELT LIKE crying, but knew if she gave in she wouldn't stop. She had to get away from Tyler and Nathaniel, they made her feel things she'd never felt before. Their sole attention had been utterly focused on her and her alone. Not once did they make her feel anything other than like a person. She'd never had that before.

She could have done without the reminder that it was her birthday, though. That meant her father would be awake when she got home, just to remind her that she was the butt of every April fool's joke, and a huge mistake. It didn't matter that she paid all the bills or for his drinking habit, he always felt it necessary to put her down any way he could, at every opportunity. How pathetic was she that she had never had a real birthday before? It was just another day in her miserable life.

She had to go back out before Fred came looking for her. So she took a couple of deep breaths, closed her eyes, and pictured a beach, to calm her nerves. Only this time the image was different, Tyler and Nathaniel were there, too. Her eyes popped open and she frowned, feeling a little confused over that image, so she went back out to check for new customers and to see if the guys needed anything.

As Keeley walked back out to the dining area, she saw that she had three more tables. She grabbed the coffee pot and started making the rounds, getting everyone settled before going back to top up Tyler and Nathaniel's coffees.

"Would you like some more? Or something to eat?" She asked hoping they wouldn't say anything about her abrupt departure a few minutes before. But, of course, she wasn't that lucky.

Nathaniel answered. "We'll both have the pancake special, please, with extra bacon. And we'd really like to take you to breakfast after your shift is done." He didn't form it as a question, more like a demand.

"I can see the wheels turning in that beautiful head of yours. Let us take you to breakfast or lunch, or maybe dinner? Your choice. Of course, we could always take you to all three. Yep, I think that one works best for us," Tyler said to her with a wink at the end.

"Dammit Ty, you're gonna overwhelm the poor girl. Back off," Nathaniel told him with a frown, marring his beautiful brown eyes.

"Thank you for the kind offer but I can't," she declined and turned to put their order in for their meals.

"Why not?" asked Nathaniel as she was half way across the room. She stopped dead in her tracks, feeling the blush working its way up her face, which, of course, made her cheeks throb. *Damn pale skin* was all she could think as she turned around, and knew that not only could they see her embarrassment, but so could everyone else as they all waited for her to answer him.

She stood there for a full minute staring at them, until she heard him... "Because this ain't no fucking dating service, that's why," Fred said as he walked up behind her and put his meaty arm around her shoulders, and cupped her tightly.

She could see the anger in Tyler and Nathaniel's faces as they stared at where Fred's hand was. They both stood up and Tyler shot a small smile her way, and that wink she was coming to love, before refocusing his attention on Fred. Nathaniel just looked pissed off and she knew she was about to get hurt again. That was all men did. Good God, was he freaking huge; bigger than she originally thought.

"Come here, Butterfly," Nathaniel told her. She started to move, thinking whatever he was about to do would be better than having Fred's stinky self glued to her the way he was. As she took her first step, Fred held onto her arm so tightly that she whimpered. Tyler and Nathaniel growled at that. Actually growled. Glaring daggers at Fred, Nathaniel walked closer, grabbed her hand so gently she thought she was dreaming, and gave one small tug so she practically flew into his chest. The strange thing for her was that the entire time, he made sure she was protected. When she hit his chest, he put one hand to the small of her back and one to the back of her neck. It was very proprietary. His large arms engulfed her, completely surrounding her. Strangely, she felt safe, and she found she really liked the way he was caressing the back of her neck with his thumb.

Turning her head with a small smile on her face, she saw Tyler looking at her with this big wolf-like grin on his, it gave her a moment of peace. She closed her eyes, just wanting to enjoy this feeling of safety that she had never felt before. She wanted to embrace it before it was gone.

"Don't ever put your dirty fucking hands on *our* woman again. Are we clear? Don't even look at her for that matter. If I ever find out that you have done anything to make Keeley uncomfortable or feel less than safe, I will come in here and personally kick your ass before having this place shut down. And then just for kicks, I'll make you lick the dirt off my shoes. We clear?" Nathaniel said all of this to Fred with such menace in his voice that Keeley couldn't help but start to shake in fear, and grip his shirt tighter. She had a hold of it just above his abs, and feeling him tighten his grip on her calmed her nerves just a little bit.

For the first time ever, she actually heard a note of fear creep into Fred's voice when he said, "Ya man, ok. I didn't know she was yours, she never said anything."

That's when Tyler got involved and admonished him. "You think that gives you the right to touch her or speak for her anytime you like?" She tried to burrow right into Nathaniel at that, because even though his voice held a note of steel in it, Tyler's had such a fierce growl that she wanted to weep from the fear this confrontation was causing in her.

"Look guys, I'm sorry, ok. Keeley, I need you here now, but tomorrow night you can have off with pay, ok? Sound fair?" She simply nodded her head, because she just knew her voice would shake if she dared try to speak. Just then she heard the ding from the kitchen bell, signaling her other table's orders were ready. Reluctantly she left the safety of Nathaniel's arms, not looking at anyone for fear that they would see just how this encounter left her. Aroused from being so close to Nathaniel, and fearful that this would only make things worse with Fred and Eleanor.

After getting the other tables their food, she waited on the guys'. While she waited, she decided that maybe she would have lunch with them. They seemed nice enough, and the idea of a hot, filling meal was too much of a temptation to just give up. With that decided, she picked up their meals and brought them to their table.

"If the offer's still open, I would like to go to lunch with you both, but could we do it tomorrow?" She requested as she put their food down on the table. With still no response, she thought maybe she had said it too quietly, only to look up and see them both gazing at her with huge smiles on their faces. Seeing their response actually caused her to do something she hadn't done, genuinely, in far too long to remember. She smiled back.

"God, you have a gorgeous smile, woman!" Nathaniel said emphatically. "Tomorrow would be fine, Butterfly."

"What time can we pick you up?" This from Tyler.

"Ummm, would it be ok if I met you somewhere?" Keeley asked, feeling embarrassed that they would see where she lived.

They both frowned before Tyler responded, "Sure, how about two p.m. at Joy's Restaurant, downtown on Main street?"

"Ok, thank you. Enjoy your meal," she said then walked over to her other tables; feeling happier than she could ever remember.

Chapter 4

A S KEELEY WAS getting ready to leave the diner, Fred walked into the break room leaning against the door jam, just watching her with a scowl and looking very angry. "That was quite the show your boys put on out there, Keeley. Make no mistake, they don't scare me, and I've been waiting for you long enough. It's time for you to pay up, girl," he sneered, slightly confusing her with his comment about paying up.

"Paying up for what? I haven't borrowed anything," she replied.

"You didn't honestly think all those meals were free, did you? You stupid, naive girl," he said coldly.

"Eleanor told me that I got one free meal a shift when she hired me, though." She was in a huge panic now. She couldn't quite hold in the shiver of fear as he took a step closer.

"Yo Fred, you gotta order supplies, I'm running out of food!" Shouted Mike, the night cook from the kitchen. When Fred turned around to shout back, Keeley grabbed her bag and made her escape, running around him and out the front door. Not paying attention until it was too late, and just wanting to get away from him, she ran right out into the pouring rain. After just a few seconds of being out there, she was soaked to the bone and shivering like crazy.

Resigned to her fate, she started to walk the ten blocks to the house she shared with her father. Not owning a warm enough jacket to keep out the chill of the rain, she kept her head down and continued on. It was nine in the morning and most of the people had already gone to work or school, so even if it wasn't raining out, the streets would have been empty and quiet. Just what she needed right now. To be left alone, so she could think about what she'd gotten herself into by accepting the date with Nathaniel and Tyler.

Hopefully, her father would pass out shortly after he berated her. He normally laid into her for about two hours or so. That would leave her the rest of the day to get the house cleaned up and try to figure out a way to avoid her father.

About three blocks from her house, Keeley wasn't paying attention when she stepped into a puddle and fell. She hit the pavement landing on her arm, with pain instantly coming from her wrist and traveling all the way up her arm. She sat there just cradling her arm to her chest for almost twenty minutes before getting up and carrying on home.

When she finally made it there, her father was up and waiting for her just like she suspected he would be. "What the hell took you so long, dumbass? You should have been home an hour ago," Mack said to her.

"I'm sorry. I had a few extra tables," she said this without thinking.

"Ah, so you have more money for me then? Go ahead, give it here."

"No father, I have no extra money, you know the tips aren't as good at night," she meekly replied while slowly starting to walk towards the hall to get to her room.

"Bullshit!" He yelled at her and got up, stumbling towards her before finally leaning against the wall and grabbing her around the throat, so tightly she could hardly breathe. She just knew she was going to have a handprint, and that Nathaniel and Tyler would see it and find out just how much of a waste of time she really was.

"Please father, I swear, I have nothing extra. Check my bag," she wheezed out when he finally let go of her throat, but not before tossing her to the floor causing her to land on her injured arm, and making her cry out.

"Shut up, bitch!" He yelled as he upended her bag, looking for the money she had hidden in her bra; knowing he'd never think to look there. He was mumbling as he dug around in her bag, about what an ungrateful little brat she was. When he finished looking through it, he got up and tossed it at Keeley telling her, "It's high time your ass moves out of here, you've been nothing but a burden since the day you were born. Nobody wanted you, and I still wish your mother had aborted you when she had the chance, instead of wasting the money on her next fix. You have five minutes to pack your stuff and leave." He went back and sat down in his chair, grabbing his bottle of vodka. Keeley was surprised at this. She didn't know what to do. She had nowhere to go, no friends. Nothing. Twenty years old and she'd just been reduced to nothing.

"I said get out!!" He yelled at her again. Scrambling up she ran into her barren room and went through a few things, grabbing a couple changes of clothes and the fairy music box her grandmother had given her on her fifth birthday. It was the only present she'd ever gotten, and the last time she had seen her Grammy. One thing to be thankful for, though, was Mack had forgotten it was her birthday.

As she was walking through the living room to the front door a few minutes later, her father looked up and snarled, "Where do you think you're going, you stupid whore?"

Stupefied at his question, because he had told her to get out just a couple minutes ago, she stuttered out, "Yo—you told me to get out."

Narrowing his eyes he bit out, "Shut the fuck up and sit down."

Sitting down, across from him, on the old couch that they'd had since she could remember, Keeley was incredibly confused by his behavior. She knew today would be bad, but he'd never tried to kick her out before, and now he was acting like he never even said it.

Sitting quietly, watching him from underneath her lashes, she tensed as he leaned toward her menacingly, with a look of intense hatred and rage in his black soulless eyes. Unprepared for his quick movement, she almost wasn't in time to duck when he threw his empty bottle of vodka at her head, missing her by just centimeters. She felt it swoosh by her hair. "Go to your fucking room and don't come back out!" He screamed at her.

Flying to her room in fear, she shut the door quietly. Grabbing the small desk chair she had and wedging it under the door handle, gave her hope it would keep him out should he decide to try to attack her at any point during the day or night.

Laying on her bed cradling her knees to her chest, she prayed for a miracle. That by the grace of God, she would make it out of her house and maybe one day, have a new life.

A better life.

AFTER ANOTHER NIGHT spent tossing and turning, thinking about the situation Keeley was in, Nate got up around dawn feeling restless. Going through his morning routine of showering, he went downstairs to find Ty already in the kitchen. He had the morning news on the small TV they had above the refrigerator, turned down low, while drinking a cup of coffee.

Grabbing a mug from the cupboard, he poured himself some coffee as well, before sitting down beside Ty at the breakfast bar. Thinking about her and how vulnerable she seemed last night, left Nate with a bad taste in his mouth. He didn't want to leave her, but knew she wasn't ready for the way he wanted to take over. To make sure she feared nothing again.

Being a Marine he was used to protecting people, making sure that they were safe. Realizing he couldn't do that with her, just yet left him cold inside. He had done three tours of duty in Iraq and Afghanistan over the years, and while he liked to think it didn't change him he knew that it had. After coming home, like many soldiers, he suffered from PTSD and nightmares from the things he'd done and seen. He wasn't too proud to admit that he needed help either, which thinking back on it was probably going to be his saving grace in regards to Keeley.

If he hadn't gotten the counseling he needed, he probably wouldn't recognize her for what she was, a chance at a fulfilling and loving future.

SITTING NEXT TO Nate, Ty was lost in thoughts about the past. He knew that in order for them to convince Keeley to give them a chance they would have to present a united front, show her that they were for real.

They thought they'd had a future once, with a woman they had meet after they got home from their first tour in the Marines. She was nice, sweet, caring, and had been open to a ménage relationship, too. They thought she'd been it for them, until they really got to know her. On the outside she was what they wanted, but on the inside she was cold. Calculating. She tried to play them against each other, make the other jealous about who she spent the most time with. It might have worked, but Ty knew that their hearts hadn't been engaged. So when they came home after their second tour and found out she'd been cheating while they were gone, neither was saddened by it. More annoyed than anything.

Ty had been relieved. He hadn't realized at the time that he wasn't happy with her, until she was gone. She tried to play Nate into thinking that she was lonely and needed someone, that it was somehow their fault she was a cheater. Thankfully, he had been less engaged with her than Ty had, so he just walked away without a backward glance.

Once they'd retired and decided to put their skills to use, they both realized how much happier they were and decided to try looking for a woman to complete them. They always knew they'd have the same type of relationship as their parents. It was a relief to know that if something ever happened to either of them, the other would be there to take care of their wife and children.

GETTING UP THE next morning, stiff from not moving all night and in fear that her father would hear her and come pounding on the door, Keeley looked at the time and realized it was later than she thought. With only a few hours to get ready before her lunch date with Nathaniel and Tyler, she got up slowly to get showered and changed into something that wasn't four sizes too big and didn't have holes, like the clothes she's usually worn. Hopefully it won't be raining like the forecast had been predicting either.

Making her way quietly out of her room, Keeley darted into the bathroom across the hall to get ready for the day. Undressing, she noticed her arm was bruised from her fall the day before, but nothing major, and the fingerprints were much more noticeable on her neck, too. With tears welling up in her eyes, she hopped into the lukewarm shower and washed up quickly. Getting dressed in something presentable was a little harder than she suspected, her clothes were old hand me downs. Nothing fit properly and it was all worn and holey. Finding a pair of jeans that hung off her hips just a little, and only had holes in the knees, then grabbing a sweater and tossing it on, she figured it would have to be good enough for now. Towel drying her hair was all she was able to do before putting it up in a ponytail.

Grabbing her bag, she went out to the kitchen to grab a drink and something quick to eat, before making the long walk to the restaurant. Stopping short when she saw her father looking in the fridge, she was torn about running out the door and staying there. Her indecision cost her.

"What the fuck are you looking at?" He barked at her.

"Nothing," she replied meekly.

Seeing the anger in his face and etched in every line of his body, Keeley started to shake in fear. "What are you shaking for, girl?" He snarled. "You scared? You should be," he said while advancing on her.

Taking a step back for every step forward he took, she hit the wall at her back. "Please don't," she pleaded.

Slamming his fists on the wall on either side of her head he had her boxed in, scaring her even more. "I'm thinking you're holding out on me with your money, huh. Time for you start making more."

"I'm not, I swear," she whispered, afraid to speak too loudly, in case she angered him more by thinking she was talking back.

"Liar!" He yelled at her making her wince. "Ya know…," he started thoughtfully, "your mama used to make good money when she was whoring herself out. Got even more when she was pregnant while doing it. Seems some men like it." Smirking at the horrified look on her face, he walked away.

In that moment, Keeley knew she had to leave and she couldn't come back, or he'd force her to become what her mother was. Resolved that it was time to leave, and with nowhere to go, she went to her room to grab her coat. Taking one last look around the dingy room, eyeing the ratty bed, stained shag carpets, and peeling wall paper, she couldn't help but feel such despair; she could hardly breathe her chest was so tight. But she did what she always did, picked up her stuff and left without a backward glance.

It was freeing and terrifying, all at the same time. She started walking towards Joy's Restaurant, and Nathaniel and Tyler.

Chapter 5

GETTING UP EARLIER than usual the next morning, Ty was filled with excitement for their date with Keeley that afternoon. Grabbing a bottle of water, he went downstairs to their home gym for his daily workout. He stopped short when he saw that Nate was already there, then he laughed, because even though they weren't twins, they often had the same thoughts and actions.

"Morning," he said to his brother as he jumped on the treadmill to warm up, while Nate was working the leg machine. Giving him a chin lift in greeting, he kept on working out. After a few minutes of silence Ty finally asked, "Do you think she'll show?"

Stopping what he was doing, Nate looked at him thoughtfully before saying, "Ya, I do. I think she's been hurt Ty, not gonna lie about it, but I think she's tougher than she looks." Dwelling on that he got back to his workout, before he started thinking about what their parents had been up to. He knew they were obviously trying to set the both of them up with her.

After an exhausting and long session, Ty had a quick shower before deciding it was time to give their mother a call, to see exactly what her meddling self was up to. Smiling at the thought, he dialed and waited for her to pick up...

"...Ok Ma, we get that but you could have just told us she was the reason you wanted us to go there. How did you come across such a shitty place anyways? I know the dads never would have let you go there willingly." Ty spoke to their mother, Amber, while Nate sat there chuckling at the conversation he was having.

"Well dear, actually it was Jackson's idea to go there. You see, when we came back from that trip we took last month to New Orleans, we saw the young woman walking into Fred and Eleanor's Diner. As she went in, this big fat ugly beast of a man was coming out and dammit boys, he grabbed her. Hard." Amber paused to take a breath and stifle back the tears that were threatening to come, as she remembered that night. "You know neither of your fathers would stand for that, nor would I."

"That was Fred that did that to her. He tried to again, last night," Nate told her clenching and unclenching his fists in anger.

"Well, I hope you boys stopped him. Keeley is such a sweet girl, it's a shame she's always got new bruises on her, though. She tries so hard to cover them up, but I still see them."

"Yes Ma, we did. Nate here made it clear that she was ours," Ty said to her with a slight chuckle.

"Well, good, I think she needs some good in her life. I suspect she's had a rough one. Well, I've got to go now.

Almost time for bridge club. Have fun on your date boys!" Amber told them, cheerfully.

"Wait a sec, you said she always has bruises? How often?" Nate asked their mother.

"Often enough that I know she's suffering at home, too. She had broken ribs when we first met her; said she fell down the stairs." Their mother sighed at that. "I just knew that wasn't the case, though. Take care of her and I'll talk to you soon. Love you both."

"Love you too, Ma," they said simultaneously, ending the call.

"SHIT!" Ty was so mad he just couldn't contain it. Someone was hurting their girl. "Do you think she has a boyfriend?"

"I don't know but we'll find out at lunch. Let's go. We're already going to be late and I don't want her thinking we aren't coming." Nate started rushing Ty.

HEADING OUT IN the rain, Nate couldn't help how angry he was, on behalf of Keeley. She was too young, too beautiful to be a victim of such abuse. All those bruises, broken ribs, and who knows what else, she's suffered in her short life. He was going to find out all of it, though. It was what he did. He worked intelligence in the Marines before he retired. Digging up information was what he did best. Not many people knew he was such a computer geek, but he was their resident tech guru in Maxwell Secures, their security firm, as well.

Driving through the streets of Austin with Ty beside him, and clenching the steering wheel, he thought about her and how she acted early yesterday morning, and he could see the signs. She was shy; only making eye contact when necessary. Skittish too; not drawing attention to herself by wearing those old ugly ass baggy clothes. He knew underneath all of it, she had a smoking hot body. His cock got hard just thinking about what she'd look like naked.

Turning onto Main Street, he was looking for a parking spot in front of Joy's Restaurant, when Ty practically sprung forward in his seat yelling, "Fuck!" Looking at what Ty was so pissed about, he noticed a small bundle of bags and what looked like a person sitting on the sidewalk just at the opening of the alley in front of Joy's, and realization dawned on him that it was Keeley.

Slamming on the brakes and throwing the truck in park, not caring that he wasn't parked legally, Nate and Ty both jumped out running for her, slowing down as they got closer to her so as not to scare the day lights out of her. Her head popped up when they were about a foot away from her, and she just looked so scared and sad. Very sad.

Crouching down beside her Ty asked, "Darlin', what are you doing out here, and what's all this stuff with you?"

Horns started blaring behind them because of the way the truck was parked, but their only concern right now was Keeley. Looking between the two of them she finally responded. "My dad kicked me out and then he made me stay, then he told me I didn't make enough money and I didn't know what to do, and I can't go back, I just can't." She said this in such a rush that Nate almost didn't catch all of it. "I didn't go inside because I just came to cancel lunch," she said this softly and with such a tone of despair that all Nate could do was sit down beside her and pull her in his lap.

"Now why would you want to cancel, Butterfly?" Knowing the subject with her dad might take her a bit to feel comfortable talking to them about.

"Well… It just didn't seem right, I don't think?" She said this like a question. Like whether she had somewhere to live or not would affect how they felt about her. Boy was she wrong.

"Come on Butterfly, why don't you give Ty your bags and he'll go park the truck, while we get a back table. I'm starving!" Surprisingly she laughed at that. A small laugh, but a laugh none the less, and it was lovely. As Nate stood up with her in his arms, he heard her suck in a sharp breath and looked down to see a pinched expression on her face. "You're in pain. What hurts?" Nate inquired.

"Nothing, I'm fine," she denied.

Nate just let her be until they got to their table. Walking into the restaurant he smiled, loving the calming atmosphere of Joy's. "Hey Nate, how are you?" Asked the hostess, Heather. She had worked there for as long as it had been open.

"I'm good Heather, a table in the back if you don't

mind, please. And bring me a first aid kit, too. Ty will be in soon."

"Ah, so this little beauty belongs to you, huh? I asked her if she wanted to come inside, but she said she was waiting on someone. Good to know it's a good someone. That arm of hers looks mighty painful. I'll get the first aid kit and pass it off to Joy, when I let her know you're here."

They followed Heather through the dining area and into the back, where they had tables reserved for private parties. It was elegantly decorated with maroon colored walls and landscape pictures of different trees from around the world hanging on them. Each picture was taken by Joy herself while she was traveling, before settling down close to her family and starting this restaurant. "I'll go grab some coffee for everyone while you wait," Heather said, leaving them alone until Ty arrived. Sitting Keeley down on a chair, Nate sat to her right and gently helped her with getting her coat off.

"Jesus sweetheart, you're soaked to the bone. Do you have anything dry in your bags?" Nate asked her as he hung her coat on the back of an empty chair. Turning around he noticed the hand print on her neck. Anger coursed through his veins knowing it had to have been her father. Running his fingers along her neck, he looked into her eyes and saw the pleading look for him to let it go.

"P…Probably not," she answered with chattering teeth and a sigh of relief that he didn't push her for answers.

"Can I see your arm? I need to know how bad the damage is please," he pleaded.

She looked at him with those gorgeous crystal blue eyes of hers searching his, for what he wasn't sure, but he hoped she found what she needed. Seemingly pleased with her assessment, she held out her left arm and he sucked in a breath. It was bruising from her wrist all the way up her arm to the sleeve of her t-shirt, where it met the elbow.

"Butterfly, what happened?" Nate asked shocked that she was still moving it without screaming in pain. He didn't think it was broken, but he still wanted Ty to take a look at it to be sure. He had been the medic on their missions overseas.

"I was walking home and slipped in a puddle and fell, the bruising is just from hitting the ground so hard. It doesn't hurts so much anymore Nathaniel." She cried so softly that if he wasn't watching, he wouldn't have known that she was.

"It'll be ok Butterfly, we'll get you all fixed up in no time," he promised her. Nate loved that she called him Nathaniel. It came out so naturally making his cock go steel hard again. He was so screwed. This tiny waif of a woman had gotten him wrapped around her little finger so fast his head should be spinning, but he found that he quite enjoyed it. Smiling, he turned when he heard the door to the room open and in walked Ty and their Aunt Joy.

"Oh dear God in heavens girl, look at that arm! Let my Ty here check it out, and you'll be good in no time at all. He was a medic in the Marines you know. One of the best there was, too!" Aunt Joy boasted proudly.

"Aunty... She doesn't need to hear my life story just yet," Ty told her with a slight blush tingeing his tanned cheeks.

Keeley had jumped when his aunt had first started talking, but she seemed to calm down once she saw that Ty was with her. It gave Nate hope. They might have only known her for a very short time, but he was glad she was starting to grow more comfortable with them.

"It's ok Tyler, I don't mind," she told them as she gave the world's smallest smile, but man alive did it ever transform her entire face. She had a slight blush on her cheeks, matching Ty's, and there was a little twinkle in her eyes like she enjoyed how proud their aunt was of their accomplishments as she bragged about them.

"Can I see your arm sweet thing, it looks like it hurts something fierce. What happened?" Ty asked her as he knelt down in front of her.

KEELEY HELD OUT her arm for Tyler to look at, trying to hide the pain she felt but knew she failed miserably when she saw their Aunt Joy's face, and the tears the nice woman was trying not to let fall on her behalf. It was weird for her, she'd never had anyone so upset over her injuries that they wanted to cry for her. "Keeley?" Tyler asked softly.

Getting back to the moment, she finally remembered he'd asked her a question. "Oh, I hurt it falling on the walk home this morning; tripped in a puddle. I landed on it when I hit the pavement, but the bruising's not so bad." She whispered that last part to herself more than anything.

"Are you sure, darlin'?" Tyler asked her this a little hesitantly, like he knew there was more to it, to her, than that.

"Yes, I am sure. It wasn't like the other times." Putting her head down, she tried to avoid their stares, sure that they were looking at her like she was some charity case. She gasped in shock as Nathaniel put his hand under her chin and lifted her head up to look him in the eyes, as Tyler started probing her arm. Sucking in a sharp breath at the pain his probing caused, she watched Nathaniel as questions formed in his beautiful brown eyes that looked just like melted chocolate. She could get lost in those them so easily. "What?" She asked him.

"Those other times?" He asked her.

Keeley felt everything freeze around her as she realized what she said. A panic started to form in her chest. It was like a vise had her lungs in their grip, and just started to squeeze. She started to hyperventilate when Nathaniel picked her up and sat her on his lap, facing Tyler. He held both of her cheeks in his hands while Nathaniel rubbed his hands up and down the tops of her thighs, and whispered in her ear. "Everything will be ok my sweet,

sweet Butterfly, nothing bad will happen to you again," he promised her as he kissed her right behind the ear. Oh, how she wanted to believe in that promise so badly.

"Darlin', look at me," Tyler told her, bringing her attention back to him. "It's going to be alright. You don't have to tell us anything yet, but we hope that when you're comfortable enough with us you will. And baby, I can't tell you how much I look forward to that day you really start to trust us, 'cause you can guarandamntee that we will always be two people you can count on." Tyler ended that beautiful statement by giving her the softest kiss imaginable. Her first kiss, too. It was soft and sweet and over far too quickly.

"Hey, don't forget me, too! And your folks, they already love this girl like their own. So you boys tread carefully." They all chuckled at Aunt Joy's outburst. Then Keeley suddenly realized what she said.

Slightly confused, she asked, "How do your parents know me?"

"Uh, well, you see... Ma and the Dads came into your restaurant one night, about a month ago, after they got back from a trip." Nathaniel stumbled out his answer.

Tyler continued where he left off. "Ma has been nagging us for the last two weeks to go in and try out the awesome pancakes, 'cause we're both suckers for a good pancake. Anyway, Ma and the Dads have been really persistent about us going, and it had to be at a certain time, too. So when we came in that night, we knew pretty quickly that it wasn't the pancakes that were so great about that crappy ass place, it was you."

Keeley just sat there a little dumbfounded. First, she wondered who their parents were, and then she wondered what was so special about her. She was just nobody with nothing going for her. What could they possibly want with her? She wondered, not really realizing she had said all of that out loud, so they could hear her. She was startled at Joy's outburst. "Now you listen here young lady, you are somebody to us. And I don't care how long it takes, you will realize this sooner or later! Got it?!" Joy told her empathically before walking out of the room. She heard Tyler and Nathaniel laughing softly, while she just sat there with her eyes wide and mouth open in shock.

"She's right, Butterfly. You are most certainly some-thing special to us," Nathaniel told her.

"Who are your parents? And why do you keep calling me Butterfly?" she asked him, still slightly shocked.

"I call you Butterfly because you remind me of one. Graceful, elegant, unique, gorgeous, vulnerable, and you could fly off the second I look away," he told her after he put her back on her chair and laid a soft kiss on her lips, like Tyler had. It was so soft that if she hadn't been watching, she wouldn't have known he'd done it. It left butterflies in her tummy, leaving a nice little hum of arousal for these two very sweet brothers that she was slowly becoming addicted to. "And your parents?" She asked when he pulled back.

"Amber, Jackson, and Andrew Maxwell. Ma said they come in almost every night," Tyler told her.

"Oh yes, I know them. Nicest people I've met in my whole life. They tip way too big though." She marveled at that.

"They just wanted to make sure you were taken care of was all," Tyler told her. "Alright darling, your arm is only sprained and bruised, some ice should help with that and limit yourself when carrying heavy things."

"But I have to work. I have to find a place to live. I don't want to go back to that shelter." She panicked.

"Calm down darlin', we'll help you figure something out. First, let's eat this marvelous meal our aunt made, and worry about the rest later, alright?" Tyler said to her as Aunt Joy brought their lunch for them.

Keeley couldn't figure them out. People were never this nice to her, like ever. She'd never known such kindness before. Never known what affection was until now. Her parents were always hitting her and talking down to her, but these men and their family were so wonderful to her, and she was a complete stranger to them. She had never been more confused in her life. There has to be a catch. *You're nobody, Keeley. They want something from you; no one is this nice for nothing.*

"Why?" She finally found the courage to ask what she was thinking.

Everyone looked at her slightly confused, not understanding. "What do you mean, why, Butterfly?" Nathaniel asked her. Oh, how she loved that nickname.

"Why are you all being so nice to me? You don't even know me. People are never this nice without wanting something in return. So I guess my real question should be, why are you being so nice to me and what do you want in return?" Blowing out a much needed breath, she waited. For what she wasn't sure, yet.

Joy came and sat down beside her, grabbed one of her hands and waited for her to look up, and when she finally did Joy spoke. "I am being nice to you because you are a nice, sweet, young woman whom I suspect has had a pretty shitty life, and I simply want it to get better. And I want to be a part of that better life. Now, what I want from you in exchange for this kindness; which is way too foreign to you for my comfort, by the way..., hmmm." Keeley held her breath waiting. "What I want from you, is simply for you to be happy. Yes, you have to be happy." Joy just smiled at her dumbfounded look before kissing her on the cheek and whispering in her ear, "I suspect these boys might have a different answer though." With a wink at her, and a stern look towards Tyler and Nathaniel, she left them alone once again.

Turning towards the men, she waited for them to talk. Finally, Tyler spoke up. "Darlin', we're being nice because it's what you deserve from everyone you meet. You have done nothing wrong to be treated the way you have been up until now, and I swear if you give me, us, a chance, we'll prove to you that we can and will take care of you."

Nathaniel interrupted him and started speaking. "We'll treat you like the princess that you are. The only thing we want from you is your trust, honesty, happiness, and a chance. We are very attracted to you and want to see where this could lead. So, instead of answering us right now, how about we eat before this food gets cold, yeah?" He squeezed her knee and nudged her towards her plate of what she now realized was one yummy looking, overly large burger and fries, cooked to perfection.

Smiling at them both she said, "I can't possibly eat all this."

"Oh, I bet you can Butterfly, give it a go and whatever you can't eat we'll take to go, alright?" Nathaniel told her.

Looking at him dubiously, she started with her fries and after the first bite dug in, wholeheartedly. They were the best fries she'd ever had. When she finished those, she looked at the burger thinking she's not gonna be able to pick it up with her arm hurting so much. Just as she was about to say something, Tyler reached over and cut it in fours so she could grab it with one hand. "Thank you," Keeley whispered with a small smile, and only feeling slightly embarrassed.

She moaned the minute the burger hit her mouth. She could taste every spice in the meat, the sauce on the bun was fabulous, and there was just enough lettuce, tomatoes, and cheese to make every bite pure perfection. Before she knew it, the meal was gone. Not even realizing she had finished, or that the guys finished before her and had been watching her eat, she felt utterly content and full. She hadn't felt full in far too long.

"Would y'all like dessert?" Joy asked as she walked in

to clear their plates away. "Maybe some coffee, too?" She inquired.

The guys looked at her for an answer. "Yes please, very much. That was the most delicious meal I've had in a really long time," she said shyly.

"Thank you Keeley, it's always a pleasure to see my food is enjoyed. I'll be back with coffee and dessert." Joy winked and left them.

"So about this no home and possibly no job thing, we would like to make you an offer, if you'll hear us out, please." Tyler implored.

"Uhm, ok, I'm listening," she told him.

"WELL, NATE AND I own our own security company, Maxwell Secures. We've had it for nearly three years now and we've been looking for a personal assistant for the last six months. Someone to handle appointments, take phone calls, come with us on meetings with old and new clients; basically, someone that can keep us on track. We both tend to get ahead of ourselves and then overbook, and well honestly, it can be a real mess. We have a secretary, but she's getting ready to retire and move closer to her grandchildren. What do you think?" Ty asked holding his breath.

"I, uh, I'm not sure I'm the right person for that job," she responded with a look of defeat that he was slightly baffled by.

"Why not, Butterfly?" Nate asked her.

"I have no experience, I have no home, hell, I don't even have an education for something like that. I was forced to drop out of school when I was fifteen to take care of everything." She sounded so dejected when she forced that out, that Ty was surprised she didn't just deflate right in front of them.

"Baby, that's ok. We wouldn't just throw you into it. You would hang around with Julia, our secretary, for a couple of months; to kind of get the lay of the land and learn about the business, and the rest we would work on together."

"But only after you let your arm heel the rest of this week, just relax a little bit, ok?" Nate interjected.

"But I'm just not good enough for something like this, I'll screw everything up. I don't even know how to use a computer. How am I supposed to do all this?"

"You'll learn darlin', and if you would like, we offer to send our employees to school for any training they require, and you could go back if you'd like. Now stop worrying," Ty told her. "About where to live; you could stay with us if you wanted, or I'm sure our folks would love to have you there, and I'd bet our Aunt Joy would love your company as well. Though I have to say, I'd really like you to stay with us, give us a chance to get to know one another better. Nate and I go back to work on Monday, so that gives us the next four days together." Putting on his most charming smile, Ty hoped she'd take them up on their offer.

Just as Keeley opened her mouth to say something,

Joy walked back in with their coffee and dessert. "Here we are, coffee for everyone and a nice warm brownie sundae just for you, dear," she said setting the dessert down in front of her. "And apple pie for the boys." With that she walked back out.

"I, uh, guess I really have no choice, huh." She didn't phrase it as a question.

"Of course you always have a choice, and we will accept whatever you choose. Whether it's what we've offered, or something you decide on your own," Nathaniel told her.

Keeley dug into her dessert with gusto, thinking over her options. She didn't want to seem too eager in accepting what they proposed, but it sounded too good to be true. So she decided that she'd make them wait. She really wanted the job, though. She was a little nervous about it but thought she was a fast learner, and as long as she had someone to follow for a while she could catch on quickly. Where to stay though was a conundrum in itself. She wouldn't go back home though; couldn't really. A shelter was out of the question, too. She had stayed at one when her parents had failed to pay the rent when she was ten years old. It was terrifying. There were other families there too, but they had some really scary people that stayed as well, and she vowed never to go back. She still remembered the day she walked in on a young girl being raped by a man. He had her mouth covered and was hurting her so badly she could hardly breathe. Keeley shuddered thinking about what would have happened if she hadn't walked in and screamed the whole place down. Everyone came running in, and thankfully that man had gone to jail, but she had never seen the girl again. She really hoped she had a better life now.

So, lost in her thoughts, she didn't realize she had finished her dessert until it was all gone. Deciding that she would accept their offer of not only the job but to stay with them as well, she felt a little better. Keeley knew it was moving fast, and maybe it wasn't wise to move in with them so quickly, but she was attracted to them and felt like maybe they were sincere in their need to keep her safe. Sipping her coffee she watched Tyler from the corner of her eye, really studying him this time. His eyes were an amazing hazel color; almost green rather than greenish-brown, but they were beautiful. He was full of muscles, too. Drool worthy. It was only four in the afternoon and he already had a five o'clock shadow, which she found really suited him. Made him even more masculine. His lips looked fuller with it, and much more kissable. With that thought, she remembered the angel soft kiss he'd given her. Not realizing what she'd done until it was too late, she had closed her eyes and put her fingers to her lips with a soft, small smile, thinking about it. About the way he smelled; like sandalwood and some spicy cologne that wasn't overwhelming but just enough to tantalize her senses, and his breath smelled faintly of mint, like he'd just brushed his teeth not long ago and coffee, really strong coffee. His lips were so soft like a feather. Hearing a strangled moan her eyes flew open in shock, and an intense blush rose up her chest and neck into her face, as she looked Tyler in the eyes. He knows was her first thought, followed closely by holy crap, the desire in his eyes was heady. His lids drooped so low she could see he was fighting this battle of desire back. What shocked her most was that it was for her. She'd never had anyone look at her like that before.

"Whatever you were just thinking about darlin', I sure as hell loved the way it made your face look. Happy, dreamy, satisfied." Tyler said that last part with a whole lot of pride, making her laugh softly at his arrogance and how right he was. Not that she'd admit it just yet.

Looking over at Nathaniel to see his reaction to Tyler's flirting, she saw he had a similar look on his face that made her think about the way he'd kissed her as well.

Eyes open this time, she remembered how he held her when she was going into panic attack mode, and how the kiss he left on the back of her ear made all kinds of butterflies flutter around her stomach. The desire that small kiss ignited in her was nothing like she had ever felt before. And if she was honest with herself, she really wanted to feel it again. Soon. When his lips touched hers shortly after that, he smelled all natural and woodsy, like he worked with fresh-cut wood a lot. His lips were slightly rougher than Tyler's, and she found she liked that, too. Nathaniel seemed like he was a little more wild and untamed than Tyler is. He had this look about him that just screamed Alpha, and he was so large, he had muscles on his muscles. His size and muscle mass should scare her, but all it did was turn her on. Looking at

Nathaniel now he looked like a predator, all growly and his eyes were pure desire, the black of his pupils taking over the brown of his irises. She felt so wanted by them, from a simple look and small touches. She loved it.

Clearing her throat and shaking off her lustful thoughts, she wanted to get back on track about the living arrangements. "So, I think if you really want me to, I'd like to stay with you both until I'm back on my feet. If that's ok, of course?"

The biggest smiles she had ever seen graced their handsome faces, and she felt a huge sense of relief that she was the one to make them so happy. Keeley found that she wanted to please them. "Of course, it's alright, darlin'! It's why we suggested it," Tyler said so enthusiastically that she couldn't help but laugh a full-on belly laugh. She was filled with a renewed sense of hope for her life.

"But first, I think we need to go shopping for some new clothes," Nathaniel told her, and before she could voice any objections, he held up his hand and said to her, "Hear me out, please." When she nodded, he continued. "You're going to need some new clothes for the job and for comfort while you heal. Ok?"

Thinking it over, she knew what he said made sense, but it didn't make accepting their help any easier. "Ok, but will you let me pay you back at least?"

Seeming to ponder this for a minute Tyler said, "How well do you cook?"

Smiling, she replied, "I love to cook!"

"Great! Then when your arm's all healed up you can cook," Tyler assured her, pleased with himself.

Chapter 6

AFTER SAYING GOODBYE to Aunt Joy, they left the restaurant and made their way to Nate's truck. He helped Keeley into the front seat, ran around to the driver's side, hopped in and started the engine while everyone buckled up. Putting the truck in gear, they started heading to one of the boutiques downtown.

"Where are we going?" She asked, unfamiliar with the route they were taking.

"Our little sister, Kennedy, works at a nice store just a few blocks away. I called her before we left, so that she'd pull a few things out for you to look through," Nate answered her.

"Oh, ok," she replied. He could tell she was feeling uncomfortable about the whole thing, and wanting to reassure her in some way, he said, "It's alright Butterfly, we want to do these things for you." Giving a reassuring smile, he caught Ty's eye at the way she smiled when he called her Butterfly.

"Here we are," Ty said a short ride later.

Parking and climbing out of the truck, they walked down the street to Bella's Boutique. Walking in, Nate forgot just how pink it really was inside. He'd been here twice before, both times to pick up their sister Kennedy, and he tried to leave quickly. The walls were a light pink and the carpets were a shaggy cream color that he couldn't begin to guess the real name of. All the clothes hangers were a light purple covered in satin fabric. The clothing were a mix of colors that he could only guess at, but probably wouldn't be accurate on any of them. "What is that smell?" Ty asked him.

"Kenny told me once it was some floral thing with vanilla," he replied dryly.

"It's Lavender and Vanilla almond," Keeley said inhaling beside them. "It reminds me of my Grammy," she whispered almost too low for them to hear. Wrapping his arm around her waist, they walked to the front of the store where there was an employee that he thought he recognized from one of his trips in.

Looking up and smiling at him and Ty, she completely ignored Keeley and asked, "Gentlemen, how can I help you today?"

Not really pleased with this woman, Nate pulled her from where she was currently trying to burrow her way into his back, placed her in front of him and said, "Well, we're here to get our girlfriend some new clothes –" Before he could finish she interrupted him saying, "Yes, of course. You're what, a size twelve?" Not waiting for a reply from anyone, she walked over to another section of the store, talking and not realizing they hadn't followed her. "We don't have much for bigger girls, but we have a few things that might be –" Turning, she finally realized they hadn't followed her, nor were they going to. Tapping her foot in impatience and almost stomping back towards them, she said, "Perhaps this store isn't for you."

Keeley looked at him with such a look of despair, all he could do was cup her cheek and whisper in her ear, "Ignore her, she's just jealous, now go look at anything you like. My sister will be out soon." Kissing her forehead, he gave her a light tap on the butt to get her going. Smiling at him, she went to a rack with some jeans on them.

"Damn, does she ever have the softest skin man," Nate whispered to Ty. "I can't wait to see what she picks out."

"Me too bro, me too." That was all either of them said for a while, as they watched her look through the rack of jeans and grab a pair.

KEELEY WAS STILL feeling overwhelmed and uncomfortable with this whole trip, but she knew they wouldn't give her any other choice. Plus, she couldn't really say no when she did, in fact, need new clothes. She could have done without the snobby employee though. She was very pretty with her long straight blonde hair, flawless tanned skin, bright green eyes, and perfect size two body. In comparison, Keeley felt frumpy. She was five feet two inches tall, and while she only weighed one hundred forty pounds she was short, so it showed.

Looking through the jeans, she found a couple of pairs for a reasonable price in her size, but were way too long on her short frame. Not seeing another employee, she was forced to ask the woman up front, who was trying to get Tyler and Nathaniel's attention but to no avail. "Umm, excuse me miss, do you have these with a shorter leg?" She asked her.

Sighing dramatically like she had interrupted her, she said, "Let me see them." Handing them over, she waited. Giving Keeley a dirty look she said, "These won't fit you, you're much too big, you need to try a bigger size and we can hem them for you."

Instantly angry, she wanted to slap this woman. Before Tyler or Nathaniel could speak up she said to her, "I think I'll wait for Kennedy before I look through anything else, and also if you could get me the manager or owner I'd appreciate it." Turning her back on the woman and the guys, she walked out the door and sat on the bench in front of the store.

Keeley knew she wasn't model thin or anything, but she didn't think a size ten was fat. And that nasty woman was implying she was huge. She'd never been so mad or insulted in her whole life. Closing her eyes and inhaling the fresh air, she just sat there enjoying the dewy afternoon, after the rain they'd had most of that morning and afternoon. The sun was shining and felt wonderful on her face.

Face in the air and feeling content, she leaned her head back only to be startled by two women sitting down on either side of her. Looking to her left the woman was older, maybe fifties, with brown hair that had just a hint of gray for streaks that she wore wonderfully. She had blue eyes that seemed to shine with happiness. This was a woman that wore her age well and enjoyed life to the fullest. Looking at the woman on her right she was startled. She looked just like Tyler and Nathaniel's mother, only with gorgeous red hair. But she had the same brown eyes and the kindest smile. Looking straight again, she waited. Not really sure what they wanted from her.

"You must be Keeley. I'm Kennedy but please call me Kenny; I'm Nate and Ty's little sister. This is my boss and owner of Bella's, Isabelle."

"It's nice to meet you both," she said shyly, not looking up.

"Well now, dear, those boys tell me you are in need of some clothes. Let's go on in there and take a look," Isabelle told her.

Before both women could stand up she said, "Um, no, it's ok. I think I'd like to stay here a little bit longer. You go on though." Once they left her alone again, with bewildered looks on their faces, she went back to enjoying the sun. Eyes closed, head back, she just breathed in the fresh air once more.

"LOOK LADY, IF you don't get your skinny ass out there and apologize to her, I'll have your job." Ty was getting sick of holding in his temper with this stuck up bitch. He kept his eyes on Keeley the whole time he argued with her. When he finally saw Kenny and Bella sit down with her, he felt an immense sense of relief that she wasn't alone, and had some nice female company.

Looking at the current problem in front of him, he let all of his anger show in his eyes and she finally realized she'd made a mistake. "I'm sorry if I insulted her, but she clearly was too big for those clothes." Turning and walking away from them she didn't think they saw the eye roll.

The ding from the bell above the door alerted them that the girls were coming in. Turning to greet them Ty didn't see Keeley. "Where's Keeley?" Nate asked before he could.

"She seems awfully upset guys, what happened?" Kenny asked them.

"Go ask the wicked bitch of the east over there. I don't know how you keep her employed here Bella. If I didn't know and love you I wouldn't recommend this place to anybody, and to be honest, if she stays I'm still not sure I will, because Christ is she mean!" Ty told her vehemently.

"You mean Veronica? That can't be right, she's sweet as pie," Bella told them.

Barking out a laugh, Nate informed her, "No way in hell is she sweet. She just told Keeley she was fat, not once but twice. And also told her that this was probably not the right store for her to shop in."

"That's why she's upset. Keeley told her that she'd wait for Kenny, and would like to speak to the manager or owner, so please do me a favor and not say anything to her. We're gonna go sit outside with her, and let's see if Veronica tells you anything or not. Ok?" Ty asked.

"Yes, yes, of course. By chance, do you know her size? Perhaps, Kenny can get some things together for her to look at in a minute?" Bella asked them.

Handing over the jeans that she had just been looking at Nate said, "She was looking to see if these had a smaller length before she walked out."

Walking out, they went and sat down beside Keeley. "How you doing, Butterfly? I'm so sorry she was such a bitch to you," Nate told her.

"I think I'd like to go home now. I don't feel very well," she replied without looking at either of them yet.

"Ah darling, don't let this bring you down. You're beautiful and there's nothing that two-faced bitch can say or do that will convince us otherwise," Ty reassured her, hoping to get some sort of response from her. A look, a smile, anything really. But he got nothing. She didn't even move.

They just sat there for about ten minutes before they heard her take a deep breath, and then she stood up. Turning towards them, she gave them a blindingly beautiful smile and said, "Let's go!" Hesitantly she grabbed their hands and pulled them towards the door of Bella's. Looking at Nate he saw the same look reflected on his brothers face that he was sure was on his own. Confused hope.

Walking into the store, she went back to the rack of jeans when they saw Kenny come from the back. "Oh goody, Keeley, come here and take a look at these clothes and see what you like," Kenny said so enthusiastically that she practically danced over.

"Uhhh, what just happened?" Ty asked Nate when the girls started grabbing clothes and going to the changing room.

"No idea, but she's smiling, so I don't care. You think Bella figured out Veronica's game?"

"Of course I did. I may be old, but I'm not a fool," Bella said walking up to them. "The girls are in the changing rooms?"

"Yes," they both replied smiling.

"Good, here, I found this, and I think it would be stunning on Keeley for a perfect night on the town." She held up a bright red halter dress that would hug her curves and flared out at the hips, and would go to about the tops of her knees. Next, she pulled out a pair of matching red sparkle peep-toe pumps with about a three inch heel. "Well, what do you think?"

"I can't wait to see her in it," Ty said.

After two hours of shopping, in which they had only grabbed three pairs of jeans, two pairs of sweatpants, five pant suits, four blouses, one pair of runners, one pair of ballet flats, and two pairs of pumps, plus the dress and pumps Bella had given them for her for a surprise, and some bra and panty sets they found while she was trying on clothes, they were on their way home. "How about pizza for dinner?" Ty asked.

"Sounds good," Nate replied.

They looked back to Keeley for her answer, only to find she'd fallen asleep with her head leaning against the window.

Half an hour later they pulled up in front of their house. It was an old Victorian-style home with a wraparound porch and gazebo on the deck, on the left side, in the front. They had added a swing to it the year before that Ty just knew Keeley was going to love. The house was a light blue color, while the porch was white. It had shutters on all the windows except the big bay window upstairs in the master bedroom, and the one in the front room. They had a very open floor plan inside, because one day they hoped to have a large family. All the remodeling and decorating had been done with a family in mind.

Ty grabbed all of her bags and went to open the front door, while Nate grabbed her from the back seat. Running up the stairs, he pulled the blankets down for her when Nate entered the room. Ty put her stuff in the walk-in closet while Nate deposited her on the bed and took off her shoes, so she'd sleep more comfortably. Stopping just to look at her, Ty felt at peace knowing this was right. That she belonged here with them. Leaving the room with the door slightly opened so she wouldn't be scared if she woke up, they headed downstairs. After calling for pizza, Ty headed into the living room with a couple of beers. Handing one to Nate, he sat down on the leather couch and just enjoyed the quiet for a while.

Chapter 7

STARTLING HERSELF AWAKE, Keeley opened her eyes and took in her surroundings. She was laying on the comfiest bed she'd ever had the pleasure of sleeping in, her body just seemed to mold to it. It was frigging huge; had to be a king. It was an older four poster bed that looked like oak, but she wasn't sure. Sitting up she looked around the room, and against one wall there were three tall dressers made of the same wood as the bed. Who needs so many dressers? Standing up she realized just how large the room was. To the left of the dressers was a very large walk-in closet that was empty, except for her new clothes and the ones she brought with her from home. Looking to the right, she saw a closed door that she assumed led to the bathroom and a huge bay window with a bench in front of it, with throw pillows all along it for sitting. Looking outside she noticed how dark it was and wondered what the time was. Deciding to grab a shower to wash off the horrible day she had, Keeley walked to the closet and grabbed a pair of sweat pants, shirt, and underwear, then headed to the bathroom.

Walking in she stopped, staring in shock at how gorgeous it was. It was all done in a beautiful white marble. The counter had three sea shell sinks in it, and there was a beautiful white oak vanity next to it. On one wall was a huge Jacuzzi tub that sat under a window that looked like it was blacked out so you could see outside, but no one could see in. The shower was at the end of the tub in its own enclosure, and it was even bigger than the tub. It had three glass walls and four shower heads that were placed in different spots all around it. It could easily fit four or five people. Hopping in the shower felt wonderful. The heads all had massagers on them that helped work the kinks out of her body.

Getting out, she quickly realized she'd have to forgo the bra for now, because she just couldn't bend her arm back without wanting to scream from the pain the movement would cause. Finished getting dressed, she walked out of the room and looking down the hall. She decided to follow the light to what she hoped would be where Nathaniel and Tyler were. Coming to what she assumed was the living room she looked around, noticing first, the huge black leather sectional couch placed in front of a brick fireplace, with a large flat screen TV mounted over top of it. Walking farther into the room, she saw the guys fast asleep on the couch with an open pizza box on the table in front of them, and a movie playing quietly on the TV in the background. Deciding to sit between them, she grabbed a pizza slice and the remote, to turn it up.

Enjoying the best pepperoni pizza she'd ever had,

Keeley realized it was her all-time favorite movie they had on, *Die Hard*. Smiling to herself, she ate two more slices before she was full and started to feel tired again. Laying down with Nathaniel just above her head and Tyler down by her feet, she felt settled, content, and most importantly safe enough to fall asleep without fear.

WAKING UP TO a grunt wasn't what Nate expected. Looking over, he noticed Keeley lying between them with her head on his leg and one arm wrapped under and around it, and she was stretched to the max so she could put her feet on Ty's lap. Looking at his brother quizzically, he mouthed the question, "What happened?"

Chuckling, Ty whispered back, "The girl's got a good kick."

Not wanting to wake her up, they both just watched her for a while, until they started to drift off again.

Not sure what woke him up this time, Nate just sat there with his eyes closed and listened. When he heard it again, he knew immediately that Keeley was having a nightmare. She was squeezing his leg so hard he felt her nails through the denim of his jeans. Next, he heard her whimpers, and even though he only had his hand on her shoulder he felt how tense her entire body was. Looking to his left to see if she'd woken Ty or not, he started to gently shake her and whisper to her, so he didn't scare her when she woke. "Butterfly, wake up. You're safe here with Ty and me."

When that didn't work, Ty started to scoot in behind her on the couch and wrapped his arms around her, while Nate got on his knees on the floor in front of her. Ty started whispering to her next. "C'mon darlin', open those amazing eyes. We're here and we won't let anything happen to you."

Waiting with baited breath, they watched her draw in a lungful of air and let out the loudest, most ear-piercing scream either of them had ever heard. Then she bolted up-right on the couch, knocking Nate on his ass and hitting Ty in the chin with her shoulder. Hyperventilating, she offered a whispered "sorry" to them both, before closing her eyes and leaning her head between her legs to breathe.

"You alright, Butterfly?" Nate asked concerned, rubbing soothing circles on her back to help her breathe through what he guessed was a rather hellish nightmare.

"I just need fresh air," was her reply before bolting to the front door and outside, setting off the house alarm they'd set after the pizza came the night before.

"I got the alarm!" Yelled Ty so that Nate could follow her outside, where he found her kneeling with her head down on the front grass, sobbing.

Sitting on the grass behind her, Nate pulled her into his arms and rocked her, not saying anything yet. Finally the alarm was off and Ty came running over, skidding down to kneel in front of her and holding her hands. It was probably a good ten minutes before she finally lifted her head and acknowledged they were there. "I'm so sorry," she apologized on a soft sob.

"Nothing to be sorry for darlin'. Wanna tell us about it?" Ty asked her.

"Not yet. I just… Can I sit here for a bit?" She asked so softly they almost didn't hear her.

"Of course. Mind if we sit with ya, Butterfly?" Nate asked.

Looking between the two of them she seemed to ponder that question for a minute, before finally answering, "I think I'd like that."

Sitting there in the quiet, they watched the sun rise on the horizon and it was breathtaking. Seeing the different shades of red, orange, and yellow turn into pinks and gold was a sight to see. Nate couldn't remember the last time he watched a sunrise just for the pure enjoyment of it. Squeezing Keeley just a little bit tighter to him, she relaxed her body and grabbed one of his hands and squeezed one of Ty's hands, before getting up and saying, "That was beautiful," with such a mind-blowing smile on her face. Nate froze and just stared at her again. He seemed to do that a lot, he thought. "Would you guys like some coffee?" She asked when she turned towards the house to go inside.

"Uh ya, sure thing, darlin," Ty said following her, leaving Nate still sitting on his ass in the early morning hours.

WALKING INSIDE THE house Keeley realized she had no

idea where the kitchen was. Stopping dead in the doorway, she got ran into from behind. "Oops, sorry darlin'." Tyler tried for remorse, but she could hear the smirk in his voice, plus his hands that he'd wrapped around her to land on her stomach.

Smiling, she turned her head to look up at him. "You don't sound very sorry, Tyler."

"You got me, I'm not. But that's only because you feel so good in my arms." Leaning down he brought his face closer to hers. So close, she could feel every puff of breath and practically feel his lips on hers. If she just stood up on her tip toes, she would surely lock lips with him.

Seeing his eyes widen in surprise, she didn't realize what was happening until her lips touched his and she was doing exactly what she had just thought. Closing her eyes she decided to enjoy the moment and his kiss. Opening her mouth, she touched her tongue to his lips and he opened his mouth and met her tongue with his own. Sighing, she let him explore her mouth the way she secretly hoped he would one day explore her body. Lifting her uninjured arm up and around to the back of his neck, she pulled his head down farther into hers. Hearing him moan she started to pull away, but he reached up and put his hand on her throat, just below her jaw holding her in place, which she enjoyed immensely. Seeing a flash go off behind her eyes, she thought nothing of it until Tyler pulled his head up and smiled at her, but it was the look in his eyes that left her wondering what was going on.

Breathless she asked, "What's with the look?"

Glancing towards Nathaniel, she saw he had a camera in his hands and an amused expression on his face. "Sorry Butterfly, I couldn't resist," he responded smiling.

Blushing, but secretly thrilled to see it she asked, "Where's the kitchen?"

Nathaniel turned to show her the way, so she followed. Entering the kitchen she was immediately in love with it. Everything matched: the fridge, stove, dishwasher, and what she assumed was a wine cooler were all stainless steel. "Geez, it all looks brand new!" She exclaimed.

The stove was a double range, the fridge had double doors with an ice dispenser on one side and the freezer in the bottom. The wine cooler was glass, so you could see inside to know how much and what was in there.

Then there was the rest of the kitchen. The cupboards on the bottom were a gleaming white with black marble tops, while the upper cupboards were the same white but had glass doors so you could see inside. It was absolutely stunning. There was a breakfast nook separating the kitchen and dining room that held the coffee maker and a hanging rack for the coffee cups. The dining room was just as stunning, yet elegantly simple. There was a matching dining table in a gorgeous cherry finish that could seat at least eight people, with a buffet and hutch to hold some very nice looking china.

"This is stunning you guys," Keeley enthused as she turned back to them, only to find they were watching her take it all in. Smiling shyly she asked where the coffee was, and got to work, as best she could with her sore arm, making it and getting everything on the breakfast bar for them. Clearing her throat she inquired, "What do you guys normally do on your days off?"

"I guess it depends on what we feel like, or what's going on around the city. Sometimes we'll go down to Dallas to catch a Cowboys or Stars game. Or hang out with the folks or Kenny. This time though we were just gonna hang out at home and do some work around here," Nathaniel told her.

Taking that in while she poured them all coffee, she thought about the job she was going to be starting soon. She was excited about this new adventure in her life. The idea that they provided security meant that they helped people, right? Lost in thought she didn't hear Tyler calling her name.

"Keeley, are you ok?" He asked.

"Oh yes, yes, I'm fine." She smiled weakly.

"What are you thinking about, Butterfly?" Nathaniel asked.

"Umm... Everything and nothing." She laughed. "I'm excited about working for you and starting fresh, but I'm really nervous about it because I've got no experience in well... anything. I didn't even finish high school, let alone be able to learn to use a computer. The only thing I've done in the last five years is waitress and clean houses. I hardly think that qualifies me for what you want me to do."

"I told you, we'll teach you and you'll have help from Julia before she retires, which won't be for a few more months. Plus, if you'd like, you can enroll in a computer course to help you learn the ins and outs of them," Tyler reminded her.

Taking a deep breath, she smiled at their generosity and asked the next question plaguing her at the moment. "You said yesterday at the restaurant that you were attracted to me, what does that mean exactly, and what do you want from me?"

Clearing his throat Nathaniel told her, "Well Butterfly, it means we like you, we feel like there could be something here for us to explore. All three of us. Ty and I both want you; and not as just some fling either. We want it all with you, do you understand?"

"I..I..I think so. You want to share me? Together?"

"Yes, baby doll. But we will never, and I mean never, make you do anything you don't want to do. We will cherish you like the princess you are. We want to take care of you," Tyler professed with the biggest smile she'd seen from him yet.

Ducking her head to take a drink of her coffee, she was equally thrilled and scared spit less at this. They were the first people to ever be kind to her, let alone want to take care of her. Tread carefully here, they could still hurt and use you. Her inner voice kept trying to interfere with what her heart wanted so badly... To be loved. It's the only thing she ever wanted and never got. Not from the parents she was forced to slave for, not from the friends she thought she had until she was forced to drop out of school, and never once from any of the seedy employers that hired her for barely minimum wage and made her do the most filthy jobs.

Deciding she wanted to get to know them better was easier said than done. She had serious trust issues, especially with men. "Would it be ok if I asked you guys some questions?"

"Anything," they both replied smiling at her.

"Ummm, gosh, I don't know where to start." Smiling sheepishly over her coffee. "How old are you both?"

"Well, I'm 32 and Ty here turned 30 not long ago," Nate responded, shocking her at their age. It didn't bother her, the age difference. She just didn't think they looked quite that old.

"Is Kennedy your only sibling?"

"You bet, thank fuck! The girl has been a pain in our asses since the day she was born! Spoilt little princess," Tyler chimed in with a smile, so she knew that while it may be true, they both still loved her very much.

"And you're Marines, right? I've heard, once a Marine always a Marine," she said it in such a gruff voice, mimicking a masculine tone that Nathaniel and Tyler both burst out laughing. "Yeah baby, that's right. Marine for life!" Tyler told her.

"How does your arm feel, Butterfly?"

"It's fine, Nathaniel. Just a little sore." She smiled at him.

Struggling with how to ask her next question, and maybe the most important one, Keeley just had to know if she was the first woman they'd shared together? Thinking about what her room looked like, she had the feeling that no she wasn't, but had they used that room with someone else? Or was she just special? Clearing her throat she mumbled out, "Have you shared women before?" Looking down and holding her breath, she waited for their answer.

"Darlin', look at me," Tyler coaxed her. Looking up, she saw their serious faces and waited. "We've shared before a few times, we like it. It makes us feel complete. But never, and I mean never, have we found a woman that we've wanted to bring home or spend more than a few nights with."

Interrupting him Nathaniel continued, "It takes a special kind of woman to be able to have this type of relationship Butterfly, and honestly, we have yet to find a woman who has wanted more than the thrill of saying she's been with two men. With you, we want it all. Everything. You understand?" He asked.

At her nod, Nathaniel went on to tell her that when they bought the house and renovated it, they knew that no woman would enter their domain until they brought home the one that would complete them. That they would marry. That even though her room was built for three, she was the only one who had ever slept in that bed. Essentially, the room was hers for as long as she was with them. It helped ease some of Keeley's anxiety, but she was still nervous. Still had doubts that they wouldn't want her once they learnt of her past. Deciding not to dwell on it anymore for now, she just enjoyed the quiet moment they were having, not prepared for their next question. She knew it was coming sooner rather than later, so she should have expected it. She just wasn't ready to trust them with those answers yet, though. Because in all honesty, who would want her when even her own parents didn't?

"Do you want to tell us what happened yesterday, before you came to the restaurant? You can trust us," Tyler implored, looking her in the eye. She saw the warmth, the concern, but she just wasn't ready. Shaking her head, she stood up and went back out the front door to sit on the swing she noticed on the porch earlier.

Chapter 8

S HE SHUT DOWN. He could see it happening as soon as the words left his mouth. Her face was devoid of emotion, and her eyes went sad before they went dead, completely. "What do we do, Nate?" He asked, not really expecting an answer, but hopeful for one none the less.

"She needs time to trust us, Ty. She'll open up when she's ready. We just need to be prepared for everything that's going to come with her story. If I had to guess, it was pure hell," Nate answered him solemnly before getting up and going to their home gym in the basement.

Ty sat there thinking for what felt like hours, but in reality was probably only twenty minutes or so, when he heard his cell phone ringing from the counter. Picking it up, he said, "Go for Maxwell."

"That crazy psycho thing you and your brother called a girlfriend, at one time, is here again Tyler Maxwell. I told you the next time she showed up I was going to sick Cooper on her. You have five minutes." Their secretary, Julia, didn't even give him a chance to reply before she hung up on him. Sighing he got up, thinking over their very, very short encounter with that viper. They should have known better than to get involved with her, she was too forward with her pursuit of them for their usual tastes. They had sex with her one time, over a year ago, and they have been avoiding her like the plague ever since. He was pretty sure she was like Lyme disease, only in human form. Once you've got it, it never leaves!

Sending a quick text to Nate that he was heading to the office to deal with something, because you don't interrupt him when he's working out, or you risk being tossed around like a sack of potatoes. He grabbed his keys and walked out the front door. Stopping in front of Keeley, he bent down and told her, "I've gotta head to the office for about an hour. Nate's downstairs in the gym, but help yourself to anything while I'm gone, alright?"

Nodding her head she finally looked at him. "Will you be gone long?"

"No baby doll, maybe an hour or so."

"Ok," she whispered back. Kissing her cheek and heading for his truck, he starts the short drive to work. Pulling up outside of their building, which is basically just an old warehouse that they had renovated to fit their security firm's needs, he saw Julia kept her word about calling in Cooper. Coop was an old Marine buddy they hired about two years ago, when he and his best friend Dane left the service. Closer than brothers, those two always stuck together.

Chuckling at the scene before him, Cooper with scratches down his face, and the viper, Tawnya, in a headlock, he couldn't help but be slightly amused.

"What's going on, Coop?" He asked, like this was an everyday occurrence, which lately it's been happening frequently enough that it almost could be.

"Same old, same old, man. Just taking out your trash." *And let the screeching commence in 3...2...* "Ahhhhhhh, I am not trash, you... you oversized ape!!! Let me go this instant, or I'm calling the police and pressing charges for assault!!!"

"Do it, you slick little viperous leech! They're on their way now to arrest YOU for trespassing and assault on poor Cooper," was Julia's smooth reply. It only knocked the wind out of her sails for about ten seconds before she started spewing her crap again.

"Cooper, you best let me go before I scream rape! And Ty, baby, how could you do this to me, to us? You, Nate, and I are soul mates. We're meant for each other!" She practically whined, only embarrassing herself further.

Getting sick of her shit, and tired of always playing nice, Ty exploded on her. "We fucked you one time Tawnya, one miserable fucking time, and honestly it wasn't even that memorable. You need to get over yourself. Accept the fact that Nate and I were done with you as soon as the condoms were off. Move the fuck on, we sure as hell have!"

"What?" She whispered venomously. Shit, he thought. "What do you mean you've moved on? You're fucking somebody else? Who the hell is she? I'll..." Cutting off her words as the police arrived, she managed to get out of Cooper's hold and was walking towards her car when the cops stopped her.

"Miss, you're going to have to come with us, please." The first officer said, while his partner was talking to Coop. "I don't think so, Officer... Adams," she purred while running her finger up and down his shirt. Thankfully the officer obviously wasn't falling for her slutty act. Slapping a cuff on one wrist while grabbing the other hand, he had her turned, cuffed, and in the back of the car in a matter of seconds. Shaking his head, the officer climbed into a very noisy car as Tawnya won't stop cussing up a storm.

With a twinge of regret for how truly fucked up that woman is, Ty walked over to Cooper and the other officer, just catching the tail end of their conversation. "...Nah man, I'm fine, just get the psycho viper out of here."

Chuckling, the officer started walking away and said, "You got it, guys."

FRUSTRATION ATE AT him as Nate was running his eighth mile on the treadmill. He wasn't sure what to do about Keeley and her fears. He knew things were bad, but the way she just turned her emotions off scared him. He worried that maybe she couldn't open up to them, tell them what has her so skittish and sad. He truly worried for her piece of mind. Twenty years old and she had the weight of the world on her shoulders. He hoped one day she would trust them enough to open up about her past.

Hearing footsteps on the stairs, he started to slow the treadmill to a steady walk. Looking up, he gave Keeley a welcoming smile and motioned her the rest of the way down with a wave of his hand. "Hey, sweet Butterfly, how are you feeling?"

Shrugging her shoulder she stepped up to the treadmill next to him, and asked with her eyes if she could go on. "Go ahead, do you know how to work it?" Shaking her head no, he stopped his and hopped off to help her turn it on to a nice steady walk. Getting back on his, they just walked, side by side, listening to the pound of their feet on the belts.

Damn, did Nate sure wish he knew what she was thinking?

A little while later, Nate could hear Ty open the front door. Keeley had to be into some deep thoughts, because she didn't move when he walked in and started coming down the stairs. It wasn't until Ty was at the bottom, and moved into her field of vision that she startled and jumped and nearly fell. Nate's quick reflexes and grabbing her upper arm is all that stopped her.

"Deep thoughts?" Ty asked her, noticing her preoccupation until she had jumped.

Shrugging again, she just said, "Not really, just thinking about what I'm going to do."

Getting an idea of where her head was at now, Nate asked her, "What do you mean? You're staying here and coming to work with us in a couple of weeks. We talked about this yesterday, Butterfly."

"I know, but I don't want to be a burden or take advantage of your kindness. I'm just..." Cutting her thoughts off, they waited to see what else she was going to say, but she just stopped.

"You just what, darlin'?" Ty tried getting her to open up.

"You guys are you; kind, open, and come from what I assume is a nice family. And I'm just... well... me... There's nothing to me. I'm nobody. I can't even remember the last time someone has been so kind to me." She whispered that last part with a huge amount of shame in her voice. "What if I fail you? Or you finally realize I'm just not worth all the effort you're trying to put into me? I'll be more broken than I am now."

Never in his life had Nate felt as hopeless as he did in that moment.

HEARING THOSE WORDS from her mouth nearly gutted Ty; he didn't know what to say. So he did what any red-blooded Texan would do—pulled her off that treadmill she hadn't stopped walking on since he startled her, and slammed his mouth down on hers. Slipping his tongue in her mouth at her gasp of surprise, he took it easy and did a slow sweep of her mouth. Leaving no crevice untouched. When she melted against him and grabbed his biceps, he knew he could finally plunder the way he wanted. She tasted like the richest chocolate, and her coffee from this morning. Putting one hand under her hair at the back of her neck and one in the small of her back, he pulled her body up and closer. Feeling her soft curves against his hard body just made his cock harder, but when she moaned and whimpered, he felt like a king.

Feeling her tense slightly, he was going to slow down and pull away until he heard Nate whisper in her ear, "You look perfect moaning into my brother's mouth Butterfly, now turn around and give me some of that sweet surrender." She didn't even hesitate, just turned and did Nate's bidding. Wrapping her arms around his neck, she whimpered and started gyrating on his brother. Pressing himself closer to her, Ty buried his face in the side of her neck and just breathed her in. She was intoxicating. When she started pulling away from Nate they let her, not wanting to overwhelm her by forcing her to do something she wasn't ready for.

"Wow." She breathed out.

"You alright, Butterfly? We didn't push you too far did we?" Nate asked her while running his hands through her dark tresses.

"No. I mean, it was nice." She smiled.

"Keeley, I need you to know that what you said, it's not true. Not to us or anybody that knows you or has ever met you. You're special. You have an inner light that's just dying to break out, but what your parents did, whatever it was, that's on them not you, never you. Ok?" Nate explained to her, cupping her cheeks and staring deeply into her eyes so she knew the words he said were one hundred percent truth. She nodded her head at him, but Nate still saw the doubt in her eyes. With that though, he saw something else, too. Something he had yet to see in her… Hope.

"C'mon, let's go make some lunch. I can hear your stomach rumbling, and Ty can tell us what was so important that he had to go into work, when we aren't due back for a few more days." Missing Ty's look of apprehension, Nate grabbed Keeley's hand to pull her upstairs. Getting her settled on a stool by the breakfast bar, Nate started pulling deli meat and everything to make a double decker sandwich out of the fridge, and put it on the counter. Grabbing a beer from the fridge he looked at Ty. Tossing it to him at his nod, Nate grabbed one for himself. "Alright Ty, start talking. What was up?"

WATCHING NATHANIEL WORK in the kitchen was one of the sexiest things Keeley had ever seen. It was only sandwiches, but watching him do something so domestic was as alluring as anything she'd ever known. She was so into watching him that she hadn't felt Tyler move in behind her until he wrapped his arms around her waist, after putting his beer bottle on the counter. Looking back at him and smiling, she went back to watching Nathaniel make lunch while Tyler told them what happened to make him go into work.

"So Julia called, and umm, Tawnya was there," Tyler revealed a little apprehensively before continuing. "She said she was going to sick Cooper on her viperous ass if I didn't hurry up."

"Oh, shit."

"Ya, dude, but that's not what I said when I got there. Coop had her in a headlock, with scratches down his face. Lord knows how that happened."

"Ok, so what happened? You weren't gone too long, so I assume the cops were called." Nate mused.

"The Lyme disease riddled bitch tried to seduce her way out of cuffs. Didn't work, thank God. But Coop didn't want to press charges, so I'm not sure what they're going to be able to do other than a restraining order."

Laughing softly at Tyler's description of the woman they're talking about she asked, "Who is she?"

Looking nervously at her, Nate put her plate with the sandwich on it down in front of her. "She was a woman we were with once, more than a year ago. She didn't mean anything to us then and she certainly doesn't now. She's a cold-hearted bitch," he said truthfully.

Tilting her head to the side and studying Nathaniel's face she said, "That seems cold. Like you used her?"

"No, sweetheart, she used us. Yes, we slept with her, but after? She lost all illusion of what we thought we saw in her, and she was nothing but greed. Demanding we give her money and buy her things. That's not what we want in a woman. Let alone one we want to spend our lives with. And no we did not, at any time, want to spend our life with her," Tyler reassured her. Shockingly, she believed them.

"She sounds like a real twatwaffle then," Keeley

mumbled before taking a bite of her sandwich. Nathaniel and Tyler just stared at her in complete shock before chuckling. "What?" She asked.

Clearing his throat and taking a drink of his beer, Nathaniel just smiled and went to get his and Tyler's plates before sitting down on her other side.

"A little surprised to hear you say something like that I guess," Tyler said before taking a huge bite of his sandwich. "You're coming out of that shell of yours and you don't even know it," he told her and smiled over to Nathaniel.

Thinking about what Tyler said, she decided then and there that she would make a concentrated effort to not only get better mentally; to understand her feelings and work through her problems, but to make Tyler and Nathaniel laugh more often. She could live off that sound alone. It soothed her soul in ways she'd never felt before.

Eating the rest of their lunch in silence, Keeley contemplated what she was going to do. She had to work, but she was very nervous about working so closely with them. They both intimidated and intrigued her, scared her and made her feel things she'd never felt before. The arousal every time one of them looked at her made her knees weak with desire. She wanted to explore these new feelings with them, but she was afraid. Afraid she wouldn't be good enough. Afraid she would scare them away with her inexperience. Afraid they only wanted her for the interim, rather than permanently, like they have implied. She had to work through these feelings of inadequacy before she could give them all of her, like they wanted.

Shaking off her nervous thoughts, Keeley decided she would have to tell them these things about her. Her fears, her hopes and dreams. She just wasn't sure how to say these things without them running off or thinking she was, what she really was, white trash. Plain and simple.

"My parents never wanted me," she blurted out, with no preamble, just ripping the band-aid off before she chickened out. "I was a mistake; that one time in a person's life that they wished they could take back, only it was too late." Looking down and picking at the rest of her sandwich she waited for a response. She wasn't sure what kind, but knew she didn't want pity. She hated pity with a passion; it was a wasted emotion, a way for people to feel bad for you but not enough to help you. Looking up when neither of them spoke, she first looked at Tyler because he was slightly more laid back, but the rage simmering in his eyes sucked the breath from her body. Keeley instinctively knew it wasn't at her, but on behalf of her.

Feeling a hand on her knee, she slowly turned to look at Nathaniel and what she saw scared her more than if he was a raging mess. He had no expression on his face. His eyes were dead, his expression gone, and his jaw was pure granite. She wasn't sure what to make of that. *Was he mad at her? That she just blurted it out? Or did he find her lacking?* Because even though they say they want her how can they, when her own parents never did?

Deciding to continue, she grabbed onto Nathaniel's hand that was on her knee and looked in his eyes. She wanted to know what he was thinking as she spoke, and told them the rest. "They reminded me daily how much they hated me. How much they wished Mom would have aborted me as soon as they found out, but they were both either too high or drunk, or both for months. When they finally sobered up and realized how much I would cost, and mess with their drugs and alcohol, it was too late." Taking a breath, Nathaniel still showed zero emotion so she continued on. "Dad used to beat Mom daily while she was pregnant, hoping that she would miscarry or I'd be a stillbirth. Unfortunately that never happened. When I was born I was supposed to be taken away, but Grammy made sure I wasn't. She insisted my parents were good people, that they could take care of me, but she never had an idea of how much trouble I was in."

"How could she not know, Keeley? Christ, how could the hospital not have known? Your mom used drugs and drank! That must have shown up on tests somewhere along the line!" Tyler screamed in outrage.

Not flinching because she expected something like that to happen, she looked at him and told them, "Sometimes, though not often, like so un-often that there's hardly no documentation on it at all, the fetus isn't affected. I was doomed from birth, because I was that one in ten million case where the baby is fine. Sure, I was underweight and much tinier than I should have been, but health wise? I was fine."

"What else happened? Why? Shit, I don't know if I want to hear anymore 'cause Butterfly, you're breaking my heart." Nathaniel whispered that last part in her ear. "How can someone not want you? Ty and I wanted you on sight!" He told her.

Turning her head, Keeley's lips connected with his. She didn't push, just rested her lips against his and savored everything that was Nathaniel. Whispering "thank you" against his lips, she deepened the kiss. Gasping when he nibbled on her lower lip, he swept his tongue inside her mouth, licking at hers while he grabbed her hips and lifted her onto his lap. One hand slid under her shirt and up her back, while the other moved up her inner thigh on her left leg. Mindful of her injured right arm she wrapped them both around his neck and pulled herself closer, so her chest was pressed against his. Her nipples were hard and rubbing against the fabric of her shirt, turning her on more. Moaning into his mouth she started nibbling on his tongue, when suddenly he growled and the hand that was on her thigh moved into her hair. He grabbed a handful and pulled back just the tiniest bit, causing a pinch of pain that shockingly turned her on more. Deepening the kiss, Nathaniel started sucking on her tongue, causing her to whimper and squirm on his lap. She heard a sound in the back of her mind, but it didn't compute until she saw the flash behind her eyelids, and Tyler's amused, "Fuck, you two are hot like that!" Keeley could just picture the grin on his face in her mind.

Pulling away from her kiss with Nathaniel she was

panting and out of breath. Feeling pretty good that he was too, she smiled and asked, "Is it supposed to keep getting better?" As the blush rose up her neck and moved into her cheeks, she hid her face in Nathaniel's very large and muscular chest, while they chuckled at her response to having her brains kissed out.

SITTING IN BED late the next evening after such a wonderful day spent with Nathaniel and Tyler just hanging out, Keeley had watched her very first soccer game too, and discovered she really enjoyed the sport. Nathaniel even promised to get her a soccer ball the next day so they could play. She just sat there for a while reflecting on her day, when she remembered she had her new clothes to put away. Getting up and going to the walk-in closet, she looked around thinking this was way too big for just her. This had to be one of the guy's room, Then she remembered them explaining it was for the three of them; that when she was ready they would share it. The closet could easily store three wardrobes. There were shoe racks on one side that could hold probably thirty pairs or more. There was what she assumed was a tie rack or maybe a scarf rack beside it. Shaking her head, she moved on to unpacking and hanging her new clothes, putting the shoes in the racks, and taking her underwear and bras to one of the three dressers in the room. Going back to the closet, she looked at the two bags she brought with her, and knew immediately she just wanted to get her music box and pictures from her Grammy out and toss the rest in the garbage. It wasn't worth keeping. Everything was old and nothing fit. There were holes and stains in everything, from over-wearing them. Deciding to leave the bags there and just grab her treasures, she made her way back over to the larger than life bed and crawled in, looking at the pictures of her and her Grammy, all of them from before her fifth birthday. Keeley missed the warmth and love she used to feel whenever her Grammy got to come around. It wasn't often because when she did, it would mean her parents had to clean up the house and themselves and act like they were a happy family. "What a lie," she whispered to herself. Putting the pictures down, she ran her fingers over the top of the music box. It was pink and purple with fairies painted all over it, in a garden. Inscribed on the front were the words 'Keeley's fairy realm for peace'. It was simple and modest, the sparkles had worn off from her constantly running her fingers all over it. But her Grammy had made it for her so she treasured it. She still remembered the day she got it.

Keeley was so excited. Today was her fifth birthday and her parents had just told her that Grammy was coming over for the day. It had been so long since she'd seen her that she thought she was going to pee her pants from excitement! Sitting on the front steps waiting for her, she finally heard the clunk, clunk of her Grammy's old car. Standing up and brushing the dirt off the butt of her dress, she waited. As soon as her Grammy's car stopped in front of the house, she ran over and screamed, "Grammy, I can't believe you're here!!" Picking her up and wrapping her in a warm hug, Keeley felt safe and loved for the first time in months.

"Of course I came Kee-bug, it's your fifth birthday! That's huge!" She whispered in her ear. "I have something for you, sweetheart." Winking, she put her down and pulled out a wrapped box from her bag.

Squealing, she started jumping up and down when her Grammy gave it to her. Sitting on the grass, she started ripping at the wrapping paper until she unveiled a sparkly box with fairies and flowers all over it. "Wow, Grammy, this is beautiful!" she exclaimed.

"Ma, why can't you wait to give her shit till you come inside?" Her mom yelled, drunkenly, from the front door. Sighing, Grammy helped her up, and together they walked in the house; Keeley with a feeling of dread, and Grammy with a smile on her face.

Kissing her mother's cheek, Grammy said hello while still holding onto her, before they made their way into the kitchen. "Mack, be a dear and go get the cake I made for Keeley, from the back seat of my car." She watched her dad go, not missing the look of anger on his face that he had to do something for her.

Hearing an "Oh, fuck" from the front door a few minutes later, Grammy ran into the living room to see the cake she'd made her smashed on the floor. "Mack Stone, you did that on purpose!" Grammy yelled at her dad. "You two think I don't notice the way my girl flinches from you both? Or how you ALWAYS reek of alcohol? I see and smell it all,"

Grammy yelled while wrinkling her nose in disgust.

"Listen here you old hag, the only reason we had this brat was because you forced Judy to have her. We never wanted the fucking little rugrat. She's too stupid to listen to anything we say, so you're damn right we're gonna punish her!" Her father, Mack, yelled back at Grammy. Running to the corner by the fridge, Keeley tried to blend in; her father always scared her when he was angry. "Get the fuck out of our house and don't come back!" Mack yelled to Grammy.

Running to her Grammy, she wrapped her arms around her waist and cried. "Please don't leave me, Grammy," she whispered before her father ripped her away by the arm, slamming the door in Grammy's face. She ran to her room and hid under her bed, because she just knew her father was coming for her.

Feeling her foot being grabbed, Keeley tried kicking out of the hold and screaming. Expecting her father, she was drug out by her mom, who flung her across the room into the wall. "No mommy, please don't," she begged before she was hit in the head so hard she blacked out. The next day she woke up and they were moving. Keeley never saw her Grammy again.

Chapter 9

NOT REALIZING SHE had cried out at her memory, Keeley was surprised to be wrapped up in Tyler and Nathaniel's arms while she cried. "I'm sorry," she whispered.

"Want to tell us what had you so wrapped up in your head you never heard us come in?" Tyler asked her while rubbing circles on her exposed stomach. Shaking her head no, she relished the feeling of safety they evoked in her. Grabbing onto each of their thighs, she pulled them both closer to her before sighing in contentment and closing her eyes.

Sometime later Keeley woke up to one of her legs thrown over Nathaniel's rock hard thigh, with his hand under her shirt and massaging her breast, while Tyler had a hand down her shorts lightly rubbing her clit. Not sure if they were awake or not, she relished the feelings going through her body. It felt like little electric shocks going from the tips of her toes all the way up her body to the top of her head. Gasping, she tried to get Tyler to rub just a little harder, and when Nathaniel pinched her nipple she went off like a rocket, her entire body tingled. Her womb tightened and she felt a gush of fluid leak from her pussy onto Tyler's hand. Enjoying the sensations too much to feel embarrassed, she watched as Tyler lifted his hand to his mouth and licked her juices off his fingers and palm, while moaning. Feeling a hand on the leg she had thrown over Nathaniel's thigh, she looked over to him when he squeezed it. "You ok, Butterfly?" He asked her. Nodding her head she gave them a big smile before Tyler moved his body between her legs, aligning his hard cock against her wet and sensitive pussy, and kissed her deeply. Arching up into him, Keeley shamelessly rubbed her sensitive breasts against his very hard and defined chest, causing her nipples to harden further. Running her hands up Tyler's sides she felt him shiver and in that moment she knew she affected him as much as they affected her. Wrapping her legs around Tyler's hips and her arms around his shoulders, she pulled him in closer to her body and moaned out long and loud.

HAVING KEELEY IN his arms was what Ty equated to heaven. She molded to him. Her soft curves were a match made for his hard angles. Slowly breaking his kiss from her she followed his lips, trying to capture them again. He started kissing down her jaw to her ear. Stopping to nibble just behind her ear, he heard her sigh and she melted into the mattress. Taking that as a sign to keep going, Ty started to move further down her body. Once he got to the pulse point on her neck he sucked gently, hearing her gasp and moan he kept moving down. Lifting her shirt, he felt Nate grab it and pull it up and over her head, while whispering to her, "You're so gorgeous laid out bare for us, Butterfly." Smiling, Ty sucked one beautiful pink nipple into his mouth and her flavor hit him like a ton of bricks; this time Ty was the one to moan out loud.

She tasted like vanilla and strawberries, and Ty was pretty sure it was her natural flavor. Letting her breast go with a pop, he moved on to the other one; sucking it in his mouth long and deep. Looking up at her muffled moan, Nate was kissing her and looked like he was inhaling her tongue. Thoroughly sucking and kissing that breast, Ty let go and moved further down her body. Reaching her shorts he looked up to see Nate and Keeley watching him. Nodding her head yes at his silent question, Ty took off her shorts and stared in awe. "Damn darlin', you've got one gorgeous pussy!" He told her reverently. They watched the blush work its way up her body, from her soft stomach all the way up to the roots of her gorgeous raven black hair.

"Now that is a truly beautiful sight," Nate remarked to her while nibbling on her neck.

"I'm a virgin," she blurted out, not really surprising either of them, but looking worried about it. "Now that is a gift to treasure for life," Ty was quick to reassure her.

"That makes me incredibly glad, Butterfly," Nate told her smiling.

Bending down Ty buried his face in her pussy and

inhaled, causing her to squeal and squirm until he started nibbling on her clit. Pulling her pussy lips apart with his fingers he licked from bottom to top, stopping to blow air on her pussy hole, making her shiver and moan. "Please," she pleaded to Ty. "Please what, darlin?" He chuckled while rubbing one finger around the opening of her pussy before pushing it in up to the first knuckle.

"Oh, my," she panted out while lifting her hips, trying to get Ty's finger in further. While he went back down for another taste, Nate sucked one nipple into his mouth and playing with her other one they sent her into overload, causing her to scream out and orgasm again. Licking up her juices, while Nate whispered in her ear how sweet that was, Ty got up to remove his shorts.

AS SOON AS Ty was up, Nate pounced between Keeley's legs. Hearing her moans of pleasure and watching her orgasm with so much abandon was one of the hottest things Nate had ever seen in his life. Feeling the bed dip on his left side, Nate looked up in time to see her eyes widen in shock at a naked Ty beside her, stroking his cock. "That's too big," she whispered sounding slightly horrified at the size of it.

Chuckling at her expression, Nate got up and removed his shorts, showing off his impressive erection, saying, "Butterfly, if you can't take Ty you won't be able to take me."

Breathless Keeley said, "I guess we know you aren't on

steroids." Looking at Nate's impressive erection.

Laughing at her humor, Nate crawled back up the bed and between her legs. Sitting back on his legs, Nate pulled her closer so her legs were draped over his and her shoulders were the only thing on the mattress. "You still doing ok, Butterfly? You say the word and we'll stop, immediately." At her nod, Nate grabbed a hold of her ass cheeks and brought her pussy to his mouth as he bent down. Wanting to get her as wet as possible, Nate sucked her clit in his mouth, while putting first one finger, then another into her pussy and spreading them as wide as he could. Feeling the spongy part of her g-spot, Nate put a just a small amount of pressure on it while biting gently on her clit. Hearing her scream and feeling the gush of liquid hit his chest, Nate realized she's a squirter. Holy fuck! *She's a dream* Nate thought to himself.

Looking up her body he saw Ty had a hold of her hair, and the top part of her body was twisted while she took her first lick of Ty's cock.

BLUSHING AT WHAT she was doing, Keeley felt on top of the world. The pleasure roaming through her body was not something she wanted to let go of anytime soon. Not sure what Nathaniel had just done to her but knowing it was a feeling she wanted again, she looked out of the corner of her eye to see some liquid running down his chest. Pausing on her way to lick Tyler's cock, she was enthralled at the way Nathaniel looked. His eyes were as dark as onyx, his body was so taught she could see the veins and muscles bulging from his head to his stomach. If it wasn't for the huge cock bobbing between his legs, she would think he was angry. "That was fucking hot as hell, Butterfly," Nathaniel told her.

"Shit, she squirts?" Tyler asked in awe. Embarrassed, Keeley buried her head in Tyler's pelvis. "Fuck, yeah," he whispered. "Come on darling, back up here. Show me what those soft pretty pink lips look like wrapped around my cock," Tyler told her. Moaning, she did exactly as he asked.

Wrapping her lips just around the head, she licked at his slit. Sucking gently, she moaned at his flavor. Salty, yet sweet, almost like coconut. Feeling Nathaniel frame her pussy with his hands she looked at him in time to see his cock rubbing her lips, moaning at the contact she sucked more of Tyler into her mouth. "Fuuuccckkkk," he moaned. "Darlin', if you don't want a mouthful of cum, you need to let go," Tyler told her breathlessly.

Wanting every part of him, she sucked him to the back of her throat and swallowed. As soon as he grabbed a handful of her hair and yanked, causing his dick to go an inch further down her throat, he came with a shout. "Mother fucker!" Swallowing his cum and slowly sucking her way back up his cock, Keeley made eye contact and what she saw stole her breath. Tyler's head was thrown back, eyes closed, and his face was a mask of complete bliss. "You did that to him," Nathaniel whispered in her ear while pushing the head of his cock in her pussy and just letting it sit there, while she stared at Tyler in awe.

Turning her head, her lips met Nathaniel's while she whispered, "I'm ready, Nathaniel," with a shy smile.

Keeley could feel the minute Nathaniel started pressing deeper inside of her. The stretch and burn of unused muscles was almost enough to make her want to yell stop. But the look on Tyler's face and the pleasure she felt when they were playing with her pussy, stopped her from calling a halt to everything. When the pressure stopped, she opened her eyes and looked into Nathaniel's. "What's wrong, why did you stop?" She asked hesitantly, afraid she'd done something wrong.

"Nothing Butterfly, well nothing you did. I forgot a condom, and it's just hard to pull out; you're so warm and tight. You feel like home," Nathaniel whispered to her while closing his eyes and taking a deep breath, preparing to pull back out.

"I get the birth control shot every three months. You don't have to... wear a condom that is. I mean I'm clean, I've never done this before." Stopping at the look on Nathaniel's face, she waited for his response with baited breath.

Slamming his mouth down on hers, Nathaniel pushed his large cock the rest of the way inside her. Tensing at the breaking of her hymen she cried out into his mouth, breaking contact, with tears streaming down her face. "Oh, gawd, that hurts," she half whined, half sobbed out, while Tyler rubbed her head and kissed her neck. Nathaniel just kept looking into her eyes, waiting for her to say go.

Seeing his arms straining and his abs clenched, Keeley knew he was holding back. Just like she knew that once he started, he would still hold back. "Please, Nathaniel? And don't hold back....anything," she implored him. Seeing the relief on his face, she knew she'd said the right thing.

He started pulling out slowly and pumping his hips back in even slower, but hitting a spot inside her that had her toes curling with each pass; she begged for more. Grabbing her legs, Nathaniel wrapped them around his hips and tangled one hand in her hair while wrapping the other under her, pushing her lower back up so he could go deeper. He really started pounding inside her, causing her to scream on each inward thrust. "Fuck me, you're so tight, Butterfly. Your pussy is so warm and just melts around my cock," he told her harshly.

When her mewling started to get louder and she was wiggling her hips more, Nathaniel looked into her eyes and asked her, "What do you need, baby? You gotta tell me."

"More, I just need... More," she gasped.

Gripping her hair tighter, he slowly moved his other hand up her body and around her chest, pinching a nipple before moving the rest of the way up and wrapping it around her neck, just under her jaw and squeezing lightly. Gasping from the new sensation, with Nathaniel's hand on her throat, Keeley could feel everything more intensely; the pleasure humming through her body was more sensitive. Having her air constricted just this little bit was both terrifying and enthralling. She could feel the pulse in her clit that much more, and her breasts felt heavier with every breath. Her womb contracting from her orgasm was much more intense. Everything was just... More. Looking into Nathaniel's eyes, she could see he really enjoyed the power he had over her pleasure from just this one move. Everything started to spiral out of control at once with that look. Lights flashed, pleasure pulsed through every cell in her body, her breath stalled then it felt like she exploded; her eyes rolled back in her head, her back arched and she dug her nails into his back on a long and loud scream while she came. He kept pounding into her pussy right through her orgasm and into another one, when he finally moaned out his own, squeezing her neck just a little tighter while coming, she came again. All Keeley could see were stars, her body was tight, and felt like it was on a cloud... pure bliss was the only way she could think to describe the feeling coursing through her veins.

With Nathaniel collapsed on top of her she couldn't move, nor did she want to. His hands still on her throat and in her hair, he rolled them to the side while his semi-hard cock slipped out and he moaned. "Jesus fucking Christ that was hot as hell, darlin'," Tyler said from behind her.

STILL TRYING TO catch his breath, Nate looked at Keeley

in wonder. Wrapping his hand around her throat was only a guess, but he remembered the way she reacted when Ty had done it in their kiss the other day. He was glad to be right that, that had been what she needed to get off. Waiting for her to open her eyes, all Nate could think was this girl is fucking perfect. She was their soul mate. He had to make sure nothing ever happened to her again.

"Butterfly, you doing ok?" Nate asked her while rubbing his hand up and down her back. Smiling at him without opening her eyes she asked, "Can we do that again?"

"I'm here and ready if you are darlin'." Ty smirked at the dreamy look on her face. Turning her over and forcing Ty onto his back, he placed his hands on her hips and pulled her on top of him. "What do I do?" She whispered.

Climbing behind her, Nate placed his hands on her ribs, leaned forward, and whispered, "I'll guide you, Butterfly," causing her to shiver. Pulling her to her knees, Ty aligned his cock with her pussy, while Nate helped her slowly lower herself onto him. Once she was fully seated on Ty, his brother moaned out, "Oh, fuck baby that is one golden pussy."

When Nate let go of her she whimpered, grabbing his hands and putting them to her breasts she told him, "Please don't leave, Nathaniel." Kissing her temple, he pressed himself to her back and his cock nestled between her ass cheeks. Moaning at the contact she started to ride up and down on Ty's cock.

HAVING KEELEY'S WARM, wet pussy wrapped around his cock, Ty felt ready to explode again. Knowing he wasn't going to last long, he grabbed her hips and slammed up into her causing her to scream, "Oh my God!"

"Come on darlin', come for me. I ain't gonna last long with that silky heat wrapped around me," Ty pleaded with her. Pumping into her faster and squeezing her hips tighter, he heard Nate ask her, "You need it again, don't ya, Butterfly."

"Yes, please," she mewled back.

Watching in fascination while Nate lifted one hand from her breast and up her torso to wrap around her throat, Nate squeezed slightly harder than before. Watching her mouth open on a silent scream and her eyes roll back in her head, combined with her pussy squeezing his cock like a vise, Ty slammed her body down onto his cock once more and came harder than he ever had before. "Fucking Christ, woman, that shit is hot as hell!" He told her once she collapsed on his chest.

"Relax Butterfly, I'm going to go run you a bath so you're not sore before you fall asleep." Nate then got up to leave. Hearing the water turn on in the bathroom, Ty started rubbing circles on Keeley's back, thinking of the way she gave herself to them. She was completely selfless, and when she came, it was like a dream. Ty couldn't remember the last time he was that turned on or affected by a woman. Seeing Nate's hand wrapped around her throat to help her reach her peak was fucking hot, too. He'd never seen anything like it before. Should have had my fucking camera he thought. He and Nate loved taking pictures of beautiful things. They'd never thought to take pictures of the women they'd been with before, but with Keeley it felt natural. He wanted to capture everything on film, so it would last a lifetime. Seeing her absolute pleasure on film would be a huge turn-on, something he could look back on in fifty years or so and remember.

When he heard the water shut off, Ty started to gently shake her. "Come on, your bath is ready, darlin'." When she just mumbled incoherently and burrowed further into his chest, he chuckled and carried her in. Placing her in Nate's lap, since he was already sitting in the tub, Ty went back to the room to change the sheets; 'cause Nate wasn't lying when he said their girl was a squirter.

LYING IN NATHANIEL'S arms after making love to him and Tyler, Keeley felt heavenly. Her body was alight with pleasure. She was a little sore between her legs but figured that was normal for her first time. Plus, her men were very large in the penis department.

Thinking about how Nathaniel wrapped his hand around her throat to get her to come, she was shocked that it hadn't scared her and, in fact, made her trust him all the more. Knowing he could do that and not hurt her was an amazing feeling. It was freeing in a way, because there were so many times when her father would try to choke her, and she figured she would be scared of such force. But all it did was turn her on more; it was like an instant way to make her orgasm. She also had doubts that maybe there was something wrong with her. Was her abuse so ingrained that she needed the violence to seek pleasure? Will they think less of her knowing she needs that to get off?

Not realizing she was mumbling about it, Keeley was shocked when Nathaniel grabbed her shoulders and turned her so she was facing him and said, "Butterfly that was fucking hot as hell. Knowing you trust me that much, to have that power and control over your mind and body, is incredibly arousing."

"You don't think there's something wrong with me? My father choked me so many times, how can I not think that I'm some kind of freak?"

Startled by Tyler's voice, she turned to look at him when he spoke. "Did it feel good, darlin'? You enjoyed what we did to you, right?"

"Yes, it was amazing. I've never felt so complete in my life."

"Then there's nothing wrong with you. If it's something you consent to and enjoy, it's natural. And believe me when I say, there was nothing sexier than seeing and feeling you let go the way did with Nate's hand around that sexy elegant throat of yours," Tyler interjected with hooded eyes and arousal in every line of his body. "Come on darlin', the bed's made and I'm wiped out."

Climbing out with his help, Keeley couldn't help but admire the solidness of his chest. The way his muscles rippled with movement as he knelt down to dry her off. Turning so he could dry her back, she watched as Nathaniel got up and out of the tub. His chest was a work of art; very defined pecs, they were solid muscle. An eight pack of abs that were so hard she could probably bounce a quarter off of him and not make a dent. His Semper Fi tattoo on the right pec was simple in calligraphy writing, but defined who he was and what he stood for. She also noticed that he had the same tattoo as Tyler on his left arm and shoulder. Brothers in Arms it read, on a waving American flag with an eagle flying over it.

"Did your whole unit have that tattoo?" she asked pointing to Nathaniel's shoulder.

"Yes, we got them done after our first tour," Nathaniel told her before picking her up and carrying her to bed. Kissing her goodnight Nathaniel climbed in beside her, laying her head on his chest and wrapping his arm around her back to settle on her ribs. Once Tyler shut off the light he climbed in behind her, kissing the back of her head and whispering goodnight, he molded his front to her back. Within minutes, Keeley fell asleep into one of the best nights of sleep she'd had in her life.

Chapter 10

FEELING BETTER THAN she had in years, both physically and emotionally, Keeley decided that she was going to make the guys dinner. After a week of staying in their home, they had finally gone back to work yesterday, and she wanted to do something nice for them. With limited mobility in her wrist still a factor, she decided on spaghetti and meatballs. Washing her hands proved to be difficult though.

Lost in thought thinking over the last week and how attentive Nathaniel and Tyler had been to her, she realized how truly happy she was here. They slept with her every night, but had yet to make a more intimate move on her again. At first she thought maybe it was because they truly did think there was something wrong with her for enjoying the way Nathaniel had wrapped his hand around her throat, but then she would see the heated looks they gave her when they thought she wasn't looking, and all the kissing left her breathless. It was amazing how just one week could change her outlook on life. How she felt stronger in their presence. When the nightmares would come from her abuse, they were there to calm her fears by telling her how much she meant to them and that it wasn't her fault. Not once did they ask about what gave her the nightmares, or why she screamed out in fear if they loomed over top of her trying to wake her up. They had to know something was very wrong but they were patient with her, which was what she needed from them and they instinctively knew that.

Not hearing the front door open or the footsteps come into the kitchen, she was startled by someone screeching, "Bitch, who the fuck are you?" Jumping, Keeley spun around in surprise and looked at the woman who just walked into Nathaniel and Tyler's house without a qualm. She was nearly six feet tall with blonde hair and blue eyes, and she would have been gorgeous except for the ton of makeup that she was wearing. Giving Keeley the worst stink eye she'd ever received, she repeated her question. "Bitch, I said, who the fuck are you and why are you in my men's house?"

Still baffled, she stuttered out hesitantly, "I'm Keeley, Nathaniel and Tyler's girlfriend." This made the woman scream bloody murder.

"No, you're fucking not!!! I am!!" Flinching as she took a few steps forward, Keeley shrunk a little and backed into the sink, while this mad woman kept advancing on her.

"Please don't," Keeley whimpered right before she hit her hard across the face, causing her to fall and land on her injured arm. Crying out she curled into a ball, which only seemed to anger her further, and she started kicking her anywhere she could land her foot. After telling her she was a useless piece of shit, she left the room. She didn't hear the front door slam shut, so she assumed this woman was still in the house. Taking a quick look around, she didn't see or hear her so she got up and bolted for the back door, and kept running until she got to the trees, and still didn't stop until her lungs were wheezing so bad she could no longer breathe.

Spotting a hollowed out tree, she crawled in and sunk down on her butt. Lifting her legs up, she hugged them to her chest and cried. *You should have known it was too good to last.* Her inner voice screamed at her.

DRIVING HOME AN hour and half later than what they told Keeley they would be, Nate had a bad feeling in his gut, and after years in the service he never ignored that feeling. "Something's wrong Ty, I can feel it," he said quietly.

"You feel it, too?" Ty asked. Nodding his head in agreement, Ty told him to step on it. Speeding through the streets of Austin to the outskirts of the city where their house was, they made it home in half the time it usually took.

Hopping out before the truck was fully stopped Ty ran to the house, with Nate close on his heels. Opening the front door quietly, with their guns pulled out from their shoulder holsters, they made their way into the house silently. Hearing clattering and a curse from the kitchen, Nate looked to Ty and motioned him forward. Walking into the kitchen on silent feet, they froze dead at the sight before them.

"What the fuck are you doing in our house?" Nate exploded at seeing Tawnya walking around the kitchen like she owned it. There was spaghetti sauce boiling over on the stove, vegetables chopped up and strewn about the counter, and about a dozen meatballs sitting in a pan on the counter uncooked, with another half-pound of meat waiting to be rounded.

Tawnya walked up to Nate like everything was normal. Kissing him on the cheek she whispered in his ear, "Welcome home, lover." Before walking over to Ty, who quickly put his hands out and told her, "Get the fuck away from me you crazy ass bitch."

Pouting, she stopped and tried flirting. "But Ty baby, I'm maki…"

Nate was done with her shit. Cutting her off and yelling, "Enough of your bullshit! What the fuck are you doing in our house, and where the fuck is Keeley?" Nate stormed toward Tawnya, seeing the rage in her eyes at the mention of Keeley, and the morph of her face into an ugly mask of jealousy. She quickly recovered and told them, "I don't know who you're talking about. I came over and unlocked the door myself. Nobody else was here." The slight smirk she had on her face told them both she was lying and did something to her.

"I'm telling you this for the last time, Tawnya," Nate snarled, getting right in her face. "We are done with you.

You were a disgusting mistake and we have zero desire to repeat it. And so help me God, if Keeley has one hair out of place or slightest mark on her body because of you, I will end you without a second thought. You understand me?" By the paling of her face, Nate thought she might finally understand that they were serious. When she nodded her head yes to his question, Nate looked to Ty and told him, "Call the cops and have her ass arrested for trespassing, and anything else you can come up with. I'll call Mom and the Dads and start searching for our girl."

Going out the opened back door, from what Nate suspected was Keeley running from Tawnya, he ran toward the woods behind their house. He paused and pulled out his cell to call his parents. "Hello," Nate's dad, Jackson, answered on the first ring.

"Dad, she's missing." That was all Nate could get out before his voice nearly cracked. He felt like his world was ripped out from under his feet. His lungs were tight, his palms were sweaty, and he was dangerously close to going back inside and strangling Tawnya.

"On our way, son." That was all his dad said before hanging up. Hearing footsteps behind him, Nate turned and saw Ty making his way towards him. "They're coming, Ty," Nate informed him.

Not waiting for a response, Nate started walking into the woods, knowing Ty would follow him. They walked in silence, listening for any sound that could possibly be from Keeley. Watching the ground and tree branches for any clues of the direction she went he asked, "Police arrested her, right?" Seeing Ty's nod he continued. "She's gonna be even more skittish now. Who knows what that viper said to her," Nate snarled.

Holding his hand up for silence, "Do you hear that?" Hearing sniffling not far ahead they both started to run. "Keeley, doll, where are you?" Ty half yelled so he didn't startle her.

"There!" Nate pointed just ahead, at a hollowed out tree, when he saw her in her white sweater from this morning; only now it was caked in dirt and leaves, looking nothing like what she had put on earlier. Slowing down as they got closer to her, they came to a stop and knelt down trying to grab her attention. She had her arms wrapped around her bent legs, and was rocking back and forth, mumbling something that they had to lean closer to hear. "You're nothing Keeley, never have been, never will be. No one could want you." His heart breaking at her words, Nate put his hand on the back of her head gently and was startled when she screamed. "Shit," he said showing Ty his hand covered in blood.

"Come on baby, let's get you out of here, shall we?" Ty asked her softly. When she finally looked up, she looked right through them like they weren't there in front of her. The light they had worked so hard to put into her eyes over the past week was gone. She was pale, her hair had twigs every which way, and blood was dripping from various scratches on her face. Grabbing her hands gently, Ty pulled her to her feet and then lifted her into his arms, cradling her to his chest as they started walking quickly back to their house.

Seeing the cops were gone and their parents still weren't there, they took her straight upstairs to their room.

LAYING HER DOWN on their bed, Ty couldn't believe the turn this day had taken. He was giving serious thought to burying Tawnya out in the woods, so she could never get her claws into or anywhere near Keeley again. "I'll undress her, if you want to start a shower," he told Nate. Not looking to see if Nate was doing that he started removing her clothes. Taking off her pants, he made note of the bruises along her legs and hips. "Fucking Christ," Ty whispered, not liking what he was seeing.

He was turning when he heard Nate come back into the room. "I grabbed the first aid kit, too," Nate informed him, placing it on the dresser before coming over to help Ty get Keeley's sweater and bra off, without jostling her too much. "Has she said anything yet?" Nate asked. Shaking his head no, Ty stared in horror at the welt marks on her ribs.

"FUCK!!" Nate yelled, causing her to jump and moan from the movement. "Sorry, Butterfly, I'm just pissed this happened to you here. Come on, let's get you in the shower," Nate was quick to reassure her. They both helped her up and walked her to the shower, Ty held her while Nate stripped down and hopped in first, before grabbing Keeley and helping her sit on the bench.

"I think I heard the door. I'm gonna go check then I'll be back to help get her cleaned up." At Nate's nod of acknowledgment, Ty ran downstairs to see his parents and sister, Kenny, walking in the front door.

"Oh Ty, what happened? Is she ok? How can I help?" His mom's rapid fire questions helped ease some of his worry. Knowing that no matter what happened, Keeley would be taken care of by his family.

Kissing his mom's cheek after shaking his fathers' hands, he whispered a thank you in her ear. "Nate's in the shower with her now. I'm gonna head on up and help him get her cleaned up, then one of us will be back down."

Heading back upstairs, Ty started to strip as soon as he shut the bedroom door. Seeing her sitting in Nate's lap, on the floor crying, ripped his heart out. Climbing in behind her, he whispered, "I'm here darlin'," before touching her back gently, so as not to startle her.

"WHY ME?" KEELEY whispered into Nathaniel's strong chest. Curling her hands into fists she started to pound on his chest. "I didn't do anything to deserve this!" She wailed. Nathaniel let her pound on him until she wore herself out, and silently wept and shook with the force of her emotions. Her whole body hurt from where that woman hit and kicked her. Then the run through the woods didn't help, and caused her to get scratches all over her body. Sitting in the hollowed out trees for a few hours didn't help with the muscle cramping either.

Hearing Tyler whisper in her ear, then touch her back, helped relax her a little more. Knowing they were both with her instead of that other woman, soothed her soul. Made her feel special and cared for. But she still felt worthless. Having it drummed into her brain for years was hard to let go of. Then when she finally feels secure with them, to have something like this happen? She felt unworthy and dirty. Logically she knew it wasn't her fault and that everyone has a past, but to know that this was someone they had seen before was scary, because she didn't measure up. Keeley couldn't help the feelings she was having, she was insecure about herself with them. Whether she measured up to what they wanted and needed in a woman, or how long they planned to keep her around for. She knew her insecurities were getting the best of her. Trying to shake off her melancholy thoughts, she sat up with a wince from her many new bumps and bruises and looked to Nathaniel and whispered, "Thank you for finding me."

Kissing him softly on the lips she smiled and turned to Tyler, putting her hand on his face she leaned forward and kissed him, too. Standing up slowly she tried to stifle the moan before it came out, but wasn't quite successful. Feeling a hand on each arm, Nathaniel and Tyler helped her the rest of the way up. "Let's get you dried off and bandaged up before we get you into bed," Tyler said softly.

Leaning down to shut the shower off, Tyler stepped

out before drying off quickly, then helping her out and wrapping a towel around her. Patting her dry softly, while Nathaniel rubbed down her hair with another towel, Keeley felt slightly better. Tapping the counter with his hand, Tyler told her to hop up before they helped her sit on it. Once they finished cleaning the small cuts on her face and moved onto her hands, she finally had the courage to ask, "Who was she?" She whispered almost too low to be heard.

Looking at each other before they answered her, and with slightly leery looks on their faces, Keeley braced herself for heartache. "That was Tawnya," was all Nathaniel said with just a little bit of anger in his voice. Thinking that over, she tried to remember the familiar name when it finally registered who she was, she felt like the wind was knocked out of her. "The twatwaffle from work?" She asked feeling slightly horrified at the confirmation that she was indeed one of their past conquests.

Chuckling at her cuteness, Tyler grabbed hold of her chin and told her, "Yes, the twatwaffle who means, and meant, nothing to us. It might sound rude, but she was just someone to pass the time with. We only spent one night with her, more than a year ago. You have nothing to worry about darlin'. We're yours and you're ours, understand?" Waiting for her nod, Tyler wouldn't let go of her chin. When she didn't confirm nor deny what he said, Nathaniel looked up with his brow furrowed, stepped between her legs and said, "You are ours, Butterfly. Absolutely nothing will change that. Ever."

Punctuating that statement with a panty melting kiss, Nathaniel grabbed both her hips with enough force to leave fingerprints on her.

Moaning into his mouth, she started to grind her heat against his very erect cock. Trying to get better friction, she wrapped her legs around his hips and her arms around his back, squeezing tighter.

When Nathaniel started to pull back, she let out a little whine. Chuckling at her response he told her, "Come on, Butterfly, our parents and Kenny are here."

Giving a blush she whispered "Oh. Why?"

"They were worried about you, baby. They wanted to make sure you're ok," Tyler reassured her. Hopping off the counter, she headed into their room to get dressed before following the guys downstairs.

Chapter 11

WALKING INTO THE kitchen with one hand on Keeley's back, Ty couldn't help but feel relieved she was ok and wasn't holding back like he assumed she would. She may have been quiet when they first found her, but she wasn't reverting back into herself like she did when they tried to talk about her dad with her a week ago.

"Oh, my dear! Are you ok?" Their mom rushed over to her and wrapped her in a tight hug. Seeing Keeley close her eyes and give a small smile, he knew this was just what she needed. No one could hug like a mom can.

"I'm ok, Amber. I promise," she whispered to their mom. "I was just surprised about her coming in the way she did. Just brings back memories, and it was easier to run from them than stay and fight with that woman and the memories, you know?"

"Oh, you poor baby. I could just slap that vile creature with a broom! I can't believe she would assault you like that," their mom practically growled. "Come, sit down and have some tea and cookies dear." She had to drag Keeley to the table to sit down.

"Keeley girl, how're you doing?" Their dad, Andrew, asked her while giving her a light hug.

Smiling, she sat down and took the cup of tea his mom handed her. "I swear I'll be ok. I have bruises on my ribs, but it's nothing I can't handle." She said it so nonchalantly that you would think it was ok for her to be beaten like she had. Nate walked over to her and picked her up, placed her in his lap, and told her while nuzzling her neck, "Butterfly, it really scares me just how accepting you are of being hit like that."

Sighing, she looked around the table like she was contemplating saying something. "I had to learn to accept it, Nathaniel. Until I came here, it was my life. Everyday. Believe me when I say I don't like that it happened any more than you do. But it happened to me every day of my life by not one, but two people," she said with tears in her eyes that started to stream down her face. "I told you my parents never wanted me. I didn't just say that in a roundabout way. They hated me, the very thought of me disgusted them, and at any given time it would make one or both of them so angry that they would start beating on me. For no reason other than I was alive."

Sitting down so he was facing her, Ty grabbed her face with both hands and rested his forehead against hers and whispered, "I'm glad as fuck that you were born. I just wish it wasn't to them." Kissing her softly and pulling away, he was glad to see her gorgeous blue eyes soften.

"Oh Keeley, I'm so sorry you never got to know the love of real parents the way we have. I'm also incredibly glad you have my brothers to take care of you now. And I'm really freaking ecstatic that I won't be the only one Ty, Nate, and the dads are harping on anymore!" Count on Kenny to lighten up a mood Ty thought, smiling at his annoying, yet incredibly perceptive sister.

Jackson got up from his chair beside their mom saying, "Alright everyone, let's get out of here so this young lady can get some sleep. She looks ready to drop." Walking over to her he gave her a hug and whispered something in her ear so only she heard, causing her to laugh a little.

After saying goodbye to everyone, they ordered some Chinese food before going into the living room and turning on the TV for something to watch. "So do you think I could come into work with you tomorrow?" Keeley asked after a few minutes.

"Are you sure you're ready for that Butterfly? Your ribs must be sore, and your arm's not fully healed yet," Nate said to her.

"I'm positive, Nathaniel. I would feel safer there, with you guys, than at home. I don't want to be here by myself after today; not yet."

Looking to Nate Ty nodded his head. If she felt safer, he would do anything she wanted. It also might be good for her to meet new people.

"Alright Butterfly, if that is what you want, but only as long as you take it easy and don't work too hard, ok?"

Squealing and jumping into Nate's lap, she started raining kisses all over his face in between saying thank you, repeatedly. Laughing at her antics, Ty felt like she was really going to be ok, and she was coming out of her shell a little more every day. "Hey, what about me darlin'?" Ty teased her.

Sharing her excitement, she jumped onto his lap and kissed him deeply. Moaning into her mouth he felt like he was home. Sucking her tongue into his mouth, he played with it before following it back into hers and sweeping his tongue all around her mouth. Pulling away when he heard the doorbell, Ty picked her up and dropped her into Nate's lap with a chuckle when she squealed again.

Paying for the food, Ty went and grabbed plates and utensils from the kitchen before walking back to the living room. Shaking his head at the two of them making out, he placed everything on the coffee table before pinching her ass, making her jump and yelp. "Food's here people, let's eat!" He laughed.

"So, when we get to work tomorrow, do people know about me? Do they know we're together? Or do they think I'm with just one of you?" She asked in a rush, making it sound like one long jumbled sentence.

"Calm down darlin', you belong to us. That means everyone knows it, too. It's not a secret now, nor will it ever be. Ok?" Ty told her hoping to calm her nerves some. Nodding her head, she started to eat while Ty and Nate talked about the hockey game that Nate had found to watch.

After they were done eating and everything was

cleaned up, it wasn't long before Keeley started nodding off. Wrapping his arm around her shoulder, Ty pulled her gently down to lay her head on his lap. Lifting her feet, Nate put them on his and started rubbing them until she passed out completely. Once he knew she was out cold, Ty brought something up that had been bugging him all evening. "We need to find out exactly what her fucking sperm donor did to her, man. The things she keeps hinting at scare me. He can't get away with this shit," he vehemently stated to Nate.

"I agree Ty, but we can't let her know we're doing it. She might protest about us stirring up the hornet's nest," Nate replied angrily. "But you're right, he can't get away with what he's done to her. He needs to know she's got real men taking care of her now, and that in the future he won't even be a passing thought to her."

NATE COULDN'T BELIEVE what Keeley had told them and her parents. *Daily beatings? On a child? Who the fuck does that?* He thought. *How could anyone harm another human being the way that she obviously had been, and for twenty goddamn years?* He couldn't just let it go. Had he known it was that bad a week ago, he would have hunted the mother fucker down already and disposed of his body in the ocean, or at the very least a desert so the coyotes could eat his remains.

It burned him that they let her leave the restaurant that first day they met her, to go home to him. "Fuck!"

He said sharply, getting up. "I need to go for a run or something, man. Get rid of this wild energy running through me," he told Ty. Nodding his head, he knew he understood.

Changing into his running shorts and shoes, Nate was out the front door in minutes; running up the drive to their property and around the bend leading to the road. He ran the quarter mile that split each house, passing house after house, knowing he was taking longer than he probably should. After he passed the fourth house, he decided it was time to turn around, but instead of running he was walking. Knowing he still wasn't in the right frame of mind.

Stopping and looking up to the sky, Nate prayed for the first time since his last tour of duty. *Please let Keeley be ok. Let her understand that we're here for her. That she means everything to us. We can't lose her, not now that we've finally found her.*

He didn't know if what he felt for her was love yet or not, but the way she made him feel he was pretty sure it was damn close to it. Not wanting to be any longer than he already was, Nate started the run back home. Passing the woods that Keeley had run into today and had been there for God knows how long, made him give a slight shutter. Had she been in there past dark, who knows what could have happened to her.

Shaking off those thoughts, he concentrated on getting home to her. Knowing she was there waiting on him, asleep or not, put a smile on his face and his running kicked into high gear. Making it to the bend just before his driveway, Nate started to run faster, with anticipation of having her in his arms again.

Once he was close enough to the house, he spotted Keeley and Ty lying on a blanket on the front grass, stargazing. The smile on her face made him wonder how often she'd been able to do that before, or if she ever had. Sighing at his thoughts, he made it close enough to them that they finally looked his way. As soon as she saw him, she jumped up and ran to him.

Bracing his feet shoulder-width apart Nate caught her, when she lunged at him. Catching her around the waist and hoisting her up so her legs wrapped around him, he smiled and said "Hello my gorgeous, Butterfly." Which caused her to giggle.

"Hi, Nathaniel," she smiled and whispered against his lips. God, he loved how she was the only one to call him by his full name, and probably the only one he would ever let.

Walking over to the blanket he knelt down beside Ty, with her still in his arms. "Star-gazing, huh? I like that. It's been awhile since I've done this. What have we found so far?"

Getting excited at what Ty had already shown her, Keeley started talking animatedly and pointing them out. "See over there, those clusters that look like a broken spatula? Tyler said that's the Big Dipper. I wonder how it got that name?" She murmured. "And that over there, where those big stars are? That's Orion's Belt. I really like that one," she smiled at him.

Lying outside under the stars for nearly two more hours, Nate had never felt such contentment before. Like he had finally found who he was meant to be with. *This must be love,* he thought to himself. *It's perfect.*

Chapter 12

AFTER SPENDING THE first half of the morning at the police station, filing charges against Tawnya for trespassing, assault, and anything else they could come up with, they finally made it to the office. Walking into the building that looked more like a warehouse, Keeley's nerves started to get the best of her. She started fidgeting with the hem of her new trench jacket. Head down and not paying attention, she almost ran into what could have been a brick wall but was really an extremely large man. Grabbing onto Nathaniel's arm and maneuvering herself halfway behind him, she peeked up at what had to be one of the tallest men she'd ever met. He had to be close to seven feet tall and easily three hundred pounds or more. With a chiseled jaw that had a five o'clock shadow on it already, she felt fear course through her entire body. When Nathaniel and Tyler shook the man's hand and introduced her, she didn't comprehend anything being said; all she could hear was the blood rushing through her veins. It wasn't until Tyler pressed his front to her back, and Nathaniel turned around and wrapped his hands around the nape of her neck that she realized she was even shaking so hard her knees knocked together.

"Butterfly, you're safe here," Nathaniel whispered to her with their foreheads pressed together. "Dane won't do anything to you. Hell, he couldn't hurt a fly if he wanted to," he smirked. Looking around Nathaniel to the man he called Dane, she looked into his nearly black eyes and saw the compassion there. He knew she was scared of him, yet he wasn't trying to intimidate her like a lot of men would. He simply stood there with kindness in his eyes and a small smile on his face, while she inspected him from head to toe. He was huge. Bigger than Nathaniel. She had never seen so much muscle packed into one person before.

Moving around her guys, she walked up to Dane. Looking up into his face she whispered, "Hi." When he wrapped her up in a hug, picking her up and spinning around in circle, she couldn't help but let out a squeal of surprise.

"You're gonna be alright here, little lady. We've got your back," Dane whispered in her ear, when he put her down.

Hearing a sound from behind her, she turned around to see an older woman with gray hair and a huge smile on her face. "Well now, you must be Keeley... I'm Julia. I've heard such wonderful things about you. Welcome to Maxwell Secures, where the men are overgrown, and hot as can be!" Julia told her causing her to laugh out loud. It was freeing to be able to laugh like this with people who didn't want to cause her harm. "Come child, let's leave these overgrown beasts to do what they do, and you and I will become better acquainted." Before Keeley could protest, Julia grabbed her hand and dragged her down the hall to what she assumed was her office.

Turning her head she saw the men with smiles on their faces and chuckling, which made her relax enough to know she would be ok with Julia for the time being. Looking around Julia's office, she admired the warmth coming from this room. The decor and atmosphere were very soothing. The walls were painted a nice light blue with small pieces of artwork hanging around, mostly birds in flight, but a few with what looked like children's drawings of wild flower fields. "Did your grandchildren make these, Julia?" She asked the older woman.

"They did. They love to paint and I find that having them here, instead of some stuffy over-priced ones, is much more relaxing," Julia replied with a proud smile on her face.

"I think they're wonderful. How old are they?"

"Eight and five, now. I can't wait to move closer; I miss my grandbabies something fierce. I don't get to see them nearly enough since my son-in-law's transfer to California two years ago."

"Oh wow, that's awfully far away. Do you have other children?"

"Nope, just the one, which makes moving there so much easier," she said with a smile. "Alright, let me show you Nate and Ty's schedule for the day, and we'll get you situated with what your role will be, sound good?"

Nodding her head, Keeley was shocked at how much she was looking forward to helping with their company. "Julia?" She asked.

"Yes, dear?"

"The guys haven't really told me much about the company. What exactly is it that they do?" she inquired tentatively.

"Oh my, ok. Well, they do it all really. It might be something as small as training security personnel for an event, or finding a missing person. Sometimes they go overseas and offer protection for dignitaries or business magnates. I suppose it just depends who needs what and where," Julia explained briefly.

"Are they in danger?" The question voiced her real fear.

"Sometimes there's a case where some danger is involved. It's not often, but they are the best at what they do and take every precaution they can to make sure everyone, including themselves, stays safe." Feeling better about it, she simply nodded and started to study the schedule Julia brought up on the computer for her.

Once she had a better idea of what they did, Keeley realized it wasn't often they left the country, which settled her nerves more. Julia showed her how to handle a new case and how to open the file for it, which was much easier than she thought it would be. After learning about the filing system, which was color coded by most urgent cases, they broke for lunch. Not realizing it was nearly one in the afternoon, meaning they'd been at it for nearly three hours already, she was starving. "Let's get you to those boys, now. I'm sure they've had to hold themselves back from coming and checking on you," Julia said while getting up and grabbing her purse and coat off the rack.

Leaving Julia's office and heading to Nathaniel and Tyler's, Keeley realized how excited she was to tell them about the things her and Julia did, and that even though she had been nervous about not having experience on a computer she found it easy to maneuver on.

"Here you are dear, I'll see you in a bit," Julia remarked leaving her standing outside their closed office door.

Knocking on the door she waited for them to answer. When Tyler opened the door looking angry and had a huge scowl on his face, she immediately backed up. Not wanting to anger him further, she meekly walked in when he gestured for her to. That is when she noticed the same anger reflected on Nathaniel's face, and she started to really get scared.

"Wh—What's going on?" she asked nervously, shifting from foot to foot, unconsciously getting closer and closer to the corner of the right wall.

"You tell us, Butterfly," Nathaniel snarled the nickname he'd given her like a curse, shattering any illusion she had that what they shared was real. With a lump the size of a baseball settling in her chest, Keeley started to shake her head in the negative not understanding what was happening.

"It's like this darlin', we've been investigating your

family all morning, only to stumble across a list of charges against you as long as my arm. Care to explain?" Tyler asked with malice in his voice.

Hanging her head in shame she didn't want to answer, they already assumed she was a horrible person. What they failed to realize was she had no choice; it was life or death. She choose to live and now she wished for death. She knew one day her offenses would come back to haunt her, but it was so long ago she refused to think about it. It was best to move past it all for her own sanity. "I'm sorry, I had n-n-no choice," she stuttered out on a weak whisper.

"No choice?" Nathaniel asked her angrily. "You always have a choice, Keeley, with everything. You chose to steal from people. To con them. To make them believe you were something you're not. Is that what you were going to do to our parents? Then later to us?" He practically yelled at her.

Keeley was shaking in not only fear, but also anger now. She didn't know what to do, what to say. She had no way to defend herself against their accusations. With tears streaming down her face she railed at them, "I had no intention of doing anything to you or your family. It was you that burst into my life, Nathaniel, not the other way around. I had no choice in conning people, because it was either do it or suffer a beating to rival all others I'd had!" She yelled at them while shaking so hard her teeth were now chattering. "You have no idea what I was forced to do so my so-called parents could feed their habits. And you know what? The beatings never stopped no matter what I did. Everything I've ever done in my life, bad or good, has been with survival in mind." Breathing heavy she took a break to stare at them. Their faces were still hard and jaded so she knew, just knew, her time in this life was over. "You know I never asked you for anything, never wanted to fall in love with one man let alone two, and you made me. Both of you. Now, I'm once again left with nothing. You act like what I did was so abhorrent, yet look at what you're both doing now," she admonished before walking out of their office door, and straight through the lobby and out the front door.

Standing in the parking lot, Keeley turned around and gave the building one last look of regret before walking away. With nowhere to go and no one to call, she was left with little option but to keep walking.

"FUCK, FUCK, FUCK!!" Nate exploded out of his chair chasing after Keeley, with Ty hot on his tail; running past a startled Julia on their way out the door. They both skidded to a stop as they saw her getting on a bus a block away. "Fuck, Keeley, wait!" He yelled hoping she'd hear him. Relief swamped him as she paused and turned half way. Looking right in his eyes, she shook her head and turned her back on them. "Get the truck, Ty!" He yelled while running back inside, stopping when he saw Julia standing by his office door looking very angry.

"You want to explain to me why I saw that girl with

tears pouring down her face, and how when she saw me she ran into traffic to get on that bus?" Julia asked impatiently, tapping her foot.

"No," Nate told her before grabbing his phone and calling Dane, then running back outside to Ty, who was waiting in the truck at the front door. Climbing in as Dane answered, he told Ty to go. "Yo man, look, I can't explain, but Keeley's gone. We're following her on a bus right now, but I think we might need back up and I really don't want to call my parents. Can you meet us? I'll text you the address."

"What the fuck did you guys do to cause her to run?" Dane asked sharply. "I only spent five minutes in that girl's company, and I know that while she might be fragile as hell, she's got a heart of gold and a spine of steel."

"We were looking into her father. He's a shitty guy who spent his life beating her, and we wanted to make him pay. But then we came across her juvie record. Its long man, all sorts of things but mostly theft and conning people." Nate tried to defend his actions, even though he felt like shit for exploding on her. He knew she wasn't doing that to them, nor had she planned to. She was just too innocent to pull something like that off. Which if he thought about it, made her perfect for it, except she was too honest. They had only just finished reading the information when she knocked on their door. It had barely sunk in, and the accusations flew out of his mouth before he could even filter them.

Silence on the other end of the line had him pulling it

away from his ear and checking to see if the call discon-
nected. Seeing that it hadn't, Nate waited for the
explosion he was sure was coming. "Text me the address,"
was all Dane said before hanging up.

"What the fuck are we going to do if she doesn't let us
apologize, Nate? We just got the info, but fuck! The look
on her face when she got on the bus almost brought me
to my knees." Ty said evenly. "What did Dane say?" He
asked as an afterthought.

"We're fucked," was all Nate said, while watching the
bus like a hawk.

NOT WANTING TO give voice to his fears Ty just drove,
following the bus in the hopes that Keeley would get off
soon. Seeing Nate texting out of the corner of his eyes, he
figured he was telling Dane where they were at now. After
following the bus for over an hour, it finally turned it's
out of service sign on. As it stopped at the bus station, Ty
put the truck in park and they both hopped out going to
the front door, waiting for her to get off.

Hearing another truck door slam shut, Ty turned to
see Dane striding their way. Ty wasn't scared of many
men, if any at all, but Dane was in a league of his own.
He was an extremely large man, standing at six feet nine
inches tall and weighing just over three hundred pounds.
He scared a lot of people with his size, but it wasn't his
size that put Ty on edge, it was his combat training that
made him a deadly weapon.

Dane stopped in front of them. "You fuckers are lucky you're my friends or I'd kill you both for this, I hope you fucking know that. Shit. I still might," was all Dane said before knocking on the bus doors, waiting for the driver to open them and boarding it. They watched him walk all the way to the back, before bending down and trying to coax Keeley to get up and go with him. After about twenty minutes of back and forth between the two, they could see Dane clearly got exasperated and just picked her up in a fireman's hold, before walking back off. Putting her down in front of them, he told them all, "You two fuckers fuck with this girl again, and you're dead. She's a hell of a lot more mule-headed than you two combined. And you, little lady...," he quieted, grabbing the back of her head gently. "Listen to what they have to say. I'll be in my truck waiting for whether you want to leave with them or me," he said before doing just that.

"You are not leaving with him, Butte—"

"Don't call me that," she snapped, interrupting Nate and shocking them both.

"Oh Butterfly, I will never stop calling you that no matter how much we fuck up, or how mad you are at us. You are and always will be my Butterfly," Nate told her. "I'm sorry we jumped on you like that Butterfly. I won't offer any excuses because none would be good enough, but let us explain what happened, please?" At her nod, they started to tell her how and what they were doing. That they were shocked from the record they found on her. They didn't have the time they needed to process the information, before she knocked on the door. When they finally finished with an apology, and promised to not jump to conclusions again and simply ask her what was going on, she still hadn't said anything to them or even looked up at them. The wait was killer. To know whether she could forgive them or not was almost Ty's undoing.

Watching her finally look up at them, she nodded her head and walked over to Dane. He couldn't believe that they had screwed up so monumentally, and so soon. Ty felt a piece of his heart leave with her, when they saw her step up onto the driver's side running board and talk to Dane for a moment, before she gave him a kiss on the cheek. As she stepped down and started walking back towards them, he felt a huge weight lifted off his shoulder. Stopping to turn and wave at Dane while he pulled away, Keeley faced them again, just staring. Scrutinizing them like one would a bug under a microscope. When she started walking forward again, they both held their breath.

"I don't know if I can forgive you yet, you hurt me. I loved you and you both hurt me so bad. You just assumed I was nothing more than a common criminal. That what I did was because I wanted to, and it wasn't. I live with the guilt of having taken that money from those people every day, when they did nothing but try to help a little girl in need of a safe place." Taking a breath she continued on, with tears in her eyes and a trembling lip. "Please believe that if I could, I would pay back every cent taken, but the fact remains that I don't even know who I stole from. My

Mom chose my mark and it was completely random."

Stepping forward Nate grabbed her up in a hug, wrapping her arms around his neck and legs around his waist. Ty then walked up to her back and pressed against her. With Nate kissing her on the left side of her neck and Ty kissing her on the right, they apologized again and just held her for a few minutes before Nate let her go, and they walked over to the truck climbing in and heading home.

Chapter 13

AFTER SUCH AN exhausting couple of days, all Keeley wanted to do was be left alone and curl up into a ball and sleep for about a week. She understood their anger to a point; she would have been shocked to learn that about someone, too, but the accusations stung. The fact that they didn't even want to listen to what she had to say, and the way they both looked at her, it hurt a lot. She wasn't lying when she said that it was easier to put it all behind her and forget about it, because if she thought about it too much the guilt overwhelmed her.

Before she was old enough to work, and even sometimes after, her parents used to make her steal and con people into believing she was homeless, so they'd give her money. It worked too, for the most part. There were times when they would offer her a place to stay, and sometimes she accepted, but if she did she knew she had to steal something valuable from them or her parents would retaliate by hitting her.

Her father used to have this really thick leather belt, and he would make her kneel on the floor and whip her bare back with it, until she bled. Thankfully, she doesn't have scars from it. Probably because the lashes never went too deep into her skin. One night when she was around eleven, she had stolen the belt and hid it the neighbor's garbage cans, about a block away. That only angered her father more, and she ended up with her first broken nose because of it. To this day she still doesn't regret it, because she knew that eventually her father would have killed her.

Sitting on the window bench in her room, Keeley thought about what Dane had said to her on the bus. *Their anger comes from the fact that they're mad that they weren't there to help you, not that you did it.* Maybe it was true, maybe it wasn't. She wanted to believe it was, but she'd been so hurt that they thought she was going to steal from them and their parents, it was hard to get past. It made her think about what they really thought about her. Did they think she was white trash? Because she was, she knew that, so how could they not?

All these questions running through her mind were giving her a migraine. Getting up she walked downstairs to see if they had any Advil. Hearing hushed voices in the kitchen, she stopped just outside of it and listened when she heard her name.

"I can't believe we almost lost her, Nate. Keeley is so much more than what she thinks. She's perfect and we nearly screwed everything up. Fuck!" Tyler nearly shouted. *He thinks I'm perfect?* She thought looking down at herself, not seeing it.

"I know man, we need to cool our heads though. Her

father has to pay for what he's done to her. Twenty years of abuse and uncertainty is unacceptable. He needs to know she's going to have a better life, and that had he treated her with respect, he would have had one, too. The selfish prick," Nathaniel said to his brother.

"How do we make her forgive us? To believe in us again? I never want to see that look on her face, it nearly killed me. She was so lost and I couldn't do anything to make it better."

"Don't worry Ty, she'll come around. We're just going have to show her that we worship the ground she walks on, that she is not only beautiful on the outside but the inside as well."

Hearing them talk about her like that soothed something inside; her anger lessened and her heart melted. Clearing her throat and walking in, she whispered a quick, "Hi".

Turning around when they heard her, huge smiles spread across their faces and she lost her breath. They were both extremely handsome men that was true, but the happiness radiating from them both at seeing her, erased any lingering doubts about whether she could move past today or not.

"You ok, Butterfly? Do you need anything?" Nathaniel asked her eagerly. Looking to Tyler she saw the eagerness to help her reflected in his eyes, as well. Not knowing where she got the bravery from, she whispered out, "You", before walking back up to their room in the hopes that they'd follow her, migraine completely forgotten.

Hearing their pounding feet on the stairs, she slowly started to strip off her shirt and shorts. She was enticingly taking off her thong, bent over slightly with her ass facing the door, when they walked in. Taking a peek over her shoulder, she saw them both frozen in the doorway, with their gazes riveted to her exposed ass and pussy. Giving a little wiggle to shake her thong the rest of the way down her legs and stepping out of it, she heard dual groans coming from them.

Walking up to the bed, Keeley bent over and slowly began to crawl to the top. Looking over her shoulder when she was half-way up, Nathaniel and Tyler were still in the same spot, so she smiled seductively and asked, "Coming?" That got them moving; stripping their clothes off as they came closer. Nathaniel stared at her with hooded eyes and a small smirk, and told her, "Don't move from that spot, Butterfly."

Seeing them strip was a huge turn-on in itself for her. Nathaniel with his wide shoulders and muscles so tense his veins were popping out. His chest was a work of art; such solid and defined pecs made her want to ride him, for the sole purpose of putting her hands on them to hold. Eyes scanning further down, her breath caught at just how large his cock was. She knew it had been big when they'd made love that first time, but seeing it with the lights on, he was magnificent. It reached his belly button, and was thicker than her wrist. She didn't think she'd even be able to wrap her hand fully around it. "Like what you see, Butterfly?" he asked with a smirk covering his sexy full lips.

Nodding her head at him, her gaze swung in Tyler's direction. He was smaller in musculature than Nathaniel, but not by much. His muscles were just as defined and no less sexy, but he was slightly less bulky than his older brother. His abs went down into a nice V that she had heard so many women talk about and lose their minds over, and now she understood the allure. When Tyler dropped his boxer briefs and his cock sprang forward, a shocked gasp left her lips at how long he was. It reached his belly button and had the slightest curve at the end. Chuckling at her shock, he said to Nathaniel, "I think she likes what she's seeing, big bro."

"Oh yeah, I think she is. You ready for us, Butterfly?" Nodding her head at them, she had one gnawing question to ask. "How big are those things? That can't be normal?" When they threw their heads back in laughter, she didn't think she'd seen a more beautiful sight. *Fully erect and naked while laughing was a very good look on them both*, Keeley thought.

"Don't think I've ever measured, darlin'," Tyler finally answered, still laughing a little.

As Nathaniel climbed on the bed in front of her, Tyler climbed on behind. Putting his hands on her ass, he lowered his head and buried his face in her pussy from behind and just inhaled, causing her to close her eyes and let out a small moan. Opening them again when she felt Nathaniel's hand in her hair, pulling back so he could slam his lips down on hers, he fucked her mouth with his tongue. Not leaving any spot untouched. Tangling his tongue with hers, she couldn't help but suck on it, causing him to moan and pull her hair harder. When he had her head pulled as far back as it could go, he left her mouth to stare down at her. "Fuck you're gorgeous laid out like this for us," Nathaniel expressed to her while he just watched her.

When Tyler made his presence known by diving into her pussy with his fingers, and sucking her clit in his mouth hard, she came instantly. Her entire being flew apart, stars burst behind her eyelids, and her body shook in the aftershock of it all.

"Fuckin' beautiful!" Tyler told her, reverently placing a kiss on each of her ass cheeks. "You ready for me, baby doll?" He asked her.

Still not able to move her head because of Nathaniel's hand in her hair, she couldn't look at Tyler to say, "Yes, please", just as he rubbed his cock head through her pussy lips making her moan deep in her throat. When he placed himself at her entrance, she thought he was going to just slam in, but he slid in slowly. She could feel the burn in her pussy, stretching to accommodate his large girth. The veins in his dick brushed against her walls, causing her body to shiver in pleasure. Closing her eyes she tried to concentrate on the feeling of his dick continuing its slow slide in, when Nathaniel pulled her hair slightly and told her, "Eyes on me, Keeley," with a dark look to his stare.

Watching Nathaniel, she got lost in his eyes that had

gone nearly black from pleasure. Realizing how turned on he was watching her get pleasured by his brother made her wetter, and when she heard Tyler's whispered, "Shit", she knew he felt it too. As she went to reach for Nathaniel's cock he shook his head and said, "Uh-uh, this is all about you, Butterfly." Smiling slightly at that, she pushed back on Tyler and squeezed her pussy muscles tight when he pushed back into her.

"Holy fuck, she's squeezing me like a damn vice," Tyler said in awe, pumping into her faster and harder with each thrust. Feeling his cock grow longer and harder, Keeley knew Tyler was going to cum soon so she arched her back, sticking her ass higher in the air and squeezed her pussy muscles tighter again. On one forceful thrust he hit her g-spot, making her scream out in rapture and cum instantly. Still trying to hold Nathaniel's stare, her eyes rolled back and glazed over in pleasure, and tingles of awareness zipped all throughout her body, making every touch sensitized. When she was coming down from her high, Tyler grabbed her hips and slammed her back on his cock, as he thrust forward as hard as he could and came long and loud inside of her.

Feeling his cock hit her cervix, and the splashes of his semen on her walls, made her have flashes of smaller orgasms jerking through her body. "Fuck woman, you're gonna be the death of me. Your pussy is fucking hot and tight, I just can't last inside of you," he whispered in her ear as he bent over her body. Feeling his cock's slight jerks with his movements had her moaning in pleasure again, from her over sensitized pussy.

When he started to pull out of her, she expected to feel a gush of liquid with it. "Hell, her greedy little cunt ate up all my cum. No dripping or anything. Fucking stunning," he said with his eyes riveted between her legs, watching to see if any liquid flowed out. When it didn't, Tyler bent down and stuck his tongue in her pussy, then licked from her ass to her clit before giving it a light suck, making Keeley try and pull away because she was that sensitive.

Crawling back up over her he kissed her passionately; sticking his tongue in her mouth so she could taste their combined juices, and it was heavenly. Musky, sweet, yet slightly tangy. Turning her head because she was out of breath she said, "Wow that was... wow."

"Yeah, baby doll, it was," he agreed.

Pushing Tyler off of her, Nathaniel grabbed her by the hair again and slowly and gently dragged her up to her knees so her chest was rubbing against his. "I think you like my hair, Nathaniel." She smiled.

"You know it, Butterfly. So soft wrapped around my hands while you're riding my cock, I think I can get used to that." He smiled at her shocked expression.

Sitting back on his heels, Nathaniel used his other hand to grab her hip and help her onto his lap. Once she was sitting on his thighs, he put his hand in the small of her back, pulled her forward, and kissed her deeply. Sweeping his tongue along her lips once she opened to him, he bit her bottom one and pulled on it, causing a slight amount of pain to blend with her pleasure. Moaning, Keeley held onto Nathaniel's biceps and squeezed, digging her nails into him.

"Please Nathaniel, please, fuck me. I need you so bad," she whimpered against his lips.

"Oh Butterfly, you beg so pretty, you got me. Lift up gorgeous," he instructed her while lining up his large cock to her pussy. Moaning and whimpering as she slid down, her head fell back with Nathaniel's hand still buried in her dark locks, and gently she started to ride him. Feeling stuffed to the brim with his huge cock, she couldn't stop the little sounds coming from her. She felt every ridge and bump on him, every pulse in his veins, the beat of his heart. Going deeper on every stroke, she picked up pace, only pausing when she felt Tyler's hands on her ass and him whispering in her ear, "Do you want us both, darlin'?"

Responding before she could think it through, "Yes, please Tyler." She was startled when she felt a cool gel on her rose bud. As he started pushing a finger inside her she stopped moving, dropped her head on Nathaniel's chest and whimpered out, "Oh Tyler, that feels so weird."

"A good weird I hope?" He asked her.

Nodding her head and waiting for him to continue, Keeley was surprised at how good it felt. How much more she wanted. When he inserted another finger, she tensed up and whimpered at the burn it caused. Once he started moving his fingers in and out and scissoring them around to stretch her, the pleasure soon followed. Lifting her head up she started kissing Nathaniel again, as Tyler slipped his fingers out and put his cock head to her opening, starting to push in. Pulling from Nathaniel's mouth, she looked over at Tyler and smiled. "More please." Even though there was a slight burn, she knew the pleasure would be insurmountable. Bearing down on him while he pushed in a little more after each pass, she moaned out loud once and he was fully seated, and she could feel his pelvis against her ass cheeks.

Testing the sensations, she squeezed her ass and pussy muscles and was shocked to hear them both curse and moan at the tightness. "Oh fuck! She's so fucking tight!" Tyler growled before biting her neck, causing her to stop squeezing and gasp. Grabbing her hands behind her back, Tyler started rocking into her as Nathaniel pulled out. Fucking her in perfect symphony, they kept a slow but steady and deep pace until she was a massive mess of need and want. Feeling her fluids leaking out of her in copious amounts, Keeley needed more. She was at a precipice where almost anything would send her over the edge.

Sensing her need Nathaniel pulled her hair back exposing her slender throat, she smiled when he wrapped his other hand around it and they started fucking her harder. The harder they thrust the tighter Nathaniel squeezed. Having her air flow constricted set her body on fire, having them pound her ass and pussy harder sent her into spasms of pure delight. "Oh, fuck!" She croaked out with the little breath she had. "Please... Harder, Nathaniel," she begged, not even sure what she was begging for, them to fuck her faster and harder, or for him to squeeze tighter?

"Say it Butterfly, tell me exactly what you want," he whispered in her ear, before biting the lobe and giving a light tug, causing her to spasm around their cocks. Hearing them both groan was music to her ears.

"More… Everything… I just need harder, please." She had no shame in begging. When they started pumping into her faster and harder at the same time, her body exploded and as she was about to scream Nathaniel squeezed her throat tighter, making her eyes roll to the back of her head. Tyler let go of her hands and she immediately grabbed onto Nathaniel's forearm, squeezing as tight as he was.

Feeling Tyler cum in her ass, the heat from his semen had her body melting against him, as he groaned and bit her neck again. While she was leaning against him, Nathaniel started fucking her harder and removed his hand from her throat for just a second, so her body came alive again until Tyler grabbed it from behind and squeezed just a little. When she was about to orgasm again, Tyler squeezed her throat so tight he cut off all her air, making her cum harder than she ever had. Closing her eyes, stars burst, her body buzzed, blood rushed so fast through her veins it was all she could hear. Shivers wracked her body from toes to hair. Every touch was sensitized.

When he slowly let go of her feeling started to return to her limbs, and she was out of breath. With a whispered, "I love you", to them, she collapsed in a heap of pleasure and passed out.

STARING DOWN AT a passed out and completely unaware Keeley, she blew his mind. Nate said those words over and over again in his head. *I love you.* Unable to help the goofy grin on his face, he looked up to see an expression of awe on Ty's. "She's pretty fucking amazing, isn't she?" Nate whispered to him, not wanting to wake her up.

"Yeah man, she sure is."

When she rolled over onto her back between them, Nate saw their handprints on her throat and felt an answering twitch in his groin. "Fuck, that's sexy as hell." He placed his hand on her collarbone and rubbed his thumb gently along the base of her throat, completely turned on. Seeing their mark on her did something to him. It woke a primal urge in him to claim her as his. It was so intense he wanted to wake her up and love her body again, but knew she needed some rest.

"She's quite the surprise, hey? Never imagined she would respond like that to choking or handling both of us so well," Ty said in amazement and wonder. "She's perfect."

He chuckled at the fact that Ty kept calling her perfect, but he was right. She was completely perfect for them. Nate would give anything to keep her happy.

Chapter 14

WAKING UP TO giggling and moaning, Ty looked over to see Nate's hand running through Keeley's hair and her on her knees bent over him, giving him a blow job. Having her ass so close to him, he couldn't help but swipe his fingers through her folds, only to find her dripping wet.

"What a way to wake up," he said getting on his knees and slipping his now hard cock inside her tight, warm pussy. Moaning, she pulled off Nate to flash a smile at him, before going back to lick up and down his dick.

Closing his eyes Ty concentrated on sliding into her gently, savoring the sweetness that was all her wrapped around him. Holding her hip in one hand and pressing the other in the middle of her back, Ty took her slow and hard. Pulling out languidly, so the curve of his cock hit her g-spot on every in and out stroke, he slammed back in, hitting her cervix and causing her to squeal with each thrust.

Opening his eyes when he heard Nate groan out his release, Ty watched her clean his cock off before laying her head on his abs and sighing. Thrusting faster into her, he let out a growl when her orgasm caused his own. Emptying inside her Ty slowly started to get up, pulling her up with him and going into the shower.

Once in there, he started washing her. Foaming up the soap between his hands he started rubbing her body down, beginning at her feet and moving up her soft slender legs, when he got to her pussy he was careful to brush his hands across her sensitive clit and lips when she let out a moan. Moving up he kissed her belly, and as he got to her breasts he started massaging them. Moving his hands around her made her giggle when he got to her sides. "Ticklish there, are you?" He smiled at her nod.

After rinsing her off, he started to massage shampoo into her inky black hair. "God, I love your hair," Ty whispered to her. Rinsing the shampoo out, he massaged conditioner in when she fell into his chest and nuzzled. Leaving a kiss on each pec, Keeley pulled back and smiled before rinsing her hair out.

Seeing Nate waiting with a towel, he helped her out. While Nate dried her off, Ty quickly washed and rinsed his hair and body, knowing they had to talk to her about last night. Ty shut the water off, and as he was drying off he heard a startled gasp leaving her mouth. Looking up he saw Nate standing behind her with his hands on her hips, and the both of them had their gazes riveted to her neck in the mirror.

Walking up beside them, he ran his finger across their combined handprint on her neck. It wasn't bruised but indented, and he felt a surge of pride knowing people would see that and know she belonged to them.

"Beautiful, isn't it?" Ty asked her. When she looked at him with tears in her eyes, he was afraid she was upset about it. Looking to Nate he saw the same worry reflected in his brothers eyes. Until she smiled. Her smile lit up the entire room, and he just knew they were going to be ok.

"I love it," she murmured. "I know that's weird. That I would want something like that. But it brings me so much pleasure to let go that way, to know I can trust you both with myself. But to see the evidence of it? It's almost as good as the real thing," she confided in them with no shame. Like a woman who was coming into her own.

"Fucking proud of you for owning this, Butterfly," Nate told her with a kiss on her lips. "I love you," he proclaimed to her, looking into her clear blue eyes and making her smile.

At Ty's touch to her chin, she turned back to look at him. "There's no way I can express how happy I am to have you in my life. I love you so much, Keeley," he said kissing her forehead.

Chapter 15

A S THE WEEKS went by, Ty was amazed at how well Keeley was settling into her role at their company. She was such a quick learner. At a point now where she knew their system and schedules better than they did, she ran circles around everyone. Julia was even contemplating leaving earlier than she originally planned.

Walking up behind her while she was making copies of a file, Ty wrapped his arms around her waist, swept her hair away from her neck, and gave her a kiss on the pulse point. "Hi love, how you doin'?"

Turning in his arms, she gave him a smile, "I'm fine, Tyler. You guys don't need to keep coming and checking on me, but since you're here, would you please take this file back with you. It's the one for Emily Baxter's stalking case." She frowned, not liking how scared the woman was, when she came in the previous day to hire them to help find her stalker.

"You got it, doll. Did she call this morning?"

"Yes, she was very scared. Someone keeps calling her in the middle of the night and breathing heavily. Who are you giving this case to, Tyler?"

"We're not sure yet. It's why we're having a meeting in a few minutes," he frowned.

"Dane and Coop would be perfect." She smiled sweetly.

Snorting at her sweet, I'm so innocent face, he replied, "Darling, they're likely to send that poor girl into a fit of terrors."

Smacking his arm lightly, she shook her head at him, handed him the file, and walked back to her desk. *Guess I'm dismissed,* he thought; amused at her.

Walking into the office he shared with Nate, he plopped down in one of the chairs in front of his desk and tossed the file on top, waiting for Nate to finish his phone call.

"Yes sir, we'll leave as soon as we can," he replied to whomever he was talking to and hung up.

"What's going on?" Ty asked him, not liking the look on his face.

"We've been hired to go to Africa with some oil tycoon, to check an oil well that's misfiring. He requested you and me, personally," Nate explained.

"When do we leave?"

"As soon as possible."

"Shit, Keeley's not gonna like it. Hell, I don't like it," Ty murmured.

"Neither do I man, but we shouldn't be gone for long. A week tops," Nate assured him. "Let's go break the news to our girl. We're going to have to hand over the meeting to Dane and Coop, for Miss Baxter's case," Nate said as they were walking out of their shared office, and back to Keeley. Seeing her bent over her desk concentrating on what she was doing, Ty couldn't help feeling slightly depressed that they had to leave her soon.

"Hey, Butterfly. Ty and I have to talk to you for a second," Nate said cautiously.

Frowning at the tone of his voice, she knew something was up. "What's wrong?"

"Nothing darlin'. We got a job and we have to leave ASAP," Ty informed her.

Seeing her face drop at the news, he felt worse than he already did. "For how long? Will it be dangerous?" She asked them, worrying her hands together.

"Shouldn't be more than a week. We're escorting some oil tycoon to Africa to check out one if his wells." Nodding her head, she gave a small smile.

"You have to leave now? What about Emily? Will someone be taking her case?" She asked them, worriedly.

"Yes, Butterfly. We're gonna hand it over to Coop and Dane before we go. We won't leave her hanging." Nate pulled her up from her chair to kiss her lips. "We'll be home before you know it. Plus, our parents and Kenny will stop by, I'm sure." Nate smiled at her.

"Come here, darlin'." Ty said while pulling her from Nate. Kissing her lips and hugging her body to him, Ty basked in her scent and the perfection that was her in his arms. "We'll call you when we can, but reception will be spotty, ok?" At her nod, he gave her another kiss before pulling away.

"Just be safe, please? I love you both." She smiled that sweet smile at them, with a little wave.

"We love you, too, Butterfly. Never doubt that," Nate reassured her before they went looking for Dane or Coop.

HAVING TO SAY goodbye to Nathaniel and Tyler, without crying, was one of the hardest things Keeley had ever done. She was going to miss them something fierce.

Almost finished with her day, Dane and Coop walked up, with Dane swinging a set of keys from his fingers. "Hey, little lady, the guys forgot to give you these before they left." He smiled big, making her suspicious. In the last three weeks, she and Dane had gotten very close. He was a great friend to have, but he struggled with how people perceived him as someone to be feared, because of his size. He treated her like a little sister, and she basked in the knowledge that she truly had a good friend in him.

"What are they for? I have my house keys," she asked still confused.

"And just how did you think you were going to get home? It's an hour's drive away. Too far to walk." Coop chuckled at her shocked face, because she truly hadn't thought about it.

"Umm, I never thought about it I guess," she replied while shutting down her computer, and almost freaking out at the prospect of how she was getting home.

"Grab your stuff and follow us," Dane told her before turning to walk out of the building, leaving her with little option but to follow them. Getting outside the sun was still shining, and traffic was starting to pick up. Seeing Dane and Coop standing by a blue Ford Explorer confused and stunned her. "That's not mine, is it? I've never owned a vehicle before," she said in awe.

"Of course, it is. You didn't think they'd leave you without transpo, did you?" Dane smirked at her.

"Well, no. I mean, I really didn't think about it."

"Get in, try it out." Coop directed, walking around the front and opening the driver's side door for her. Climbing in she instantly fell in love with the cream colored leather seats and interior; it had a sunroof and automatic everything. She was also happy to note it wasn't manual. She had told them last week that she could drive, but not to ever expect her to drive a stick shift. She'd crash.

"It's mine?" She asked quietly before squealing out, "It's mine!!" in her excitement.

When Dane handed her the keys, she immediately started it up and unrolled all the windows and turned the music on. "Alright little lady, before you go, it has an automatic starter, alarm, and GPS; in case you get lost and we have to come rescue you." Dane joked. "Now drive safe and call either of us for anything at any time, you got me?"

Nodding her head she blew them each a kiss and took off. Loving the power in the engine and how quiet it was, she decided to take a drive to the mall instead of going home to a quiet house. Seeing a pet store beside the mall,

Keeley decided to stop in; seeing the puppies always made her smile.

Walking in, she immediately felt the air conditioning and gave a slight shiver. Walking over to where the dogs were, she saw so many different puppy breeds. Laughing at their antics, she walked closer and watched them through the glass.

One of the workers in the back caught her eye. She was with a medium sized dog that didn't look like it belonged here, and was about to pass it off to someone else. Keeley knocked on the glass lightly to get their attention. Waving for one of them to come over, the worker left the dog with the other person and indicated for them to wait. Coming out she asked, "How can I help you, ma'am?"

"What are you doing with that dog?" She inquired without taking her eyes off it.

Sighing, the woman told her sadly, "He's a pit bull, and someone just dropped him off this morning, by tying him up to the doors. We had to call the Humane Society to come get him, and because we have no background on him they're mostly likely going to put him down." When she said that the dog turned to look at them like he knew his fate was death. Making eye contact with her, Keeley knew she couldn't let that happen.

On impulse she said, "I'll take him. Just tell me what I have to do."

"I'm afraid it doesn't work that way, miss," she told her sadly.

"Well let's make it. I can tell you're not happy about what they're going to do to him. Help me give him a home. I want this dog. I will not accept his fate," she implored with more strength than she thought she had. *Huh, guess the guys are wearing off on me,* she thought to herself.

Smiling slightly, the woman said to her, "I'll see what I can do." Going back in, she went over to the Humane Society worker and started talking animatedly to him about what she wanted. When he looked at the dog and then up at her, and the fact the dog hadn't looked away from her, he nodded his head and handed the dog back to the pet store worker, and left through the back door.

Coming back out to Keeley with the dog in tow, she said, "Our vet is still here, let's bring him in and do a few short tests to see if he is compatible with you and has no health problems, and then we'll go from there, ok?"

Nodding her head, Keeley bent down and offered her hand to the dog, who at first was leery, but then he sniffed her hand and walked right into her body. Almost knocking her over, he nuzzled his nose into her neck before sitting down and sighing. Smiling at the worker she said, "I don't care what it takes, he's coming home with me today."

Getting up they walked to the vets office, where she had a smile on her face. "Hello dear, I watched you both from the window, and I'd say you're both perfect for each other. Let's just get a few pesky tests out of the way, to be sure he's going to be ok and has no diseases, and you can both be on your way."

As the vet did her tests, she and the worker did some shopping for him, getting a bed, toys, food, treats, and anything else they could find that they thought he might need.

After they had taken everything out to her new SUV and were walking back in, the vet and her new dog were walking out. He immediately started to whine and walk to her. Bending down to grab his leash, she gave him a pat on the head and asked the vet, "Is he ok? Can I take him home now?"

"All is well dear. He's about five years old, would be my guess, and all his tests came back negative. I gave him the vaccine's he would need for the year. The only thing he'll need now is a name," she said smiling at her.

Shaking their hands she smiled and said, "Thank you so much for this, my boyfriends just left for the week and I really only came in to see the puppies, but this guy just called to me," she told them. "I think I'll call him Rowdy." She smiled down at him as they walked out, and made their way to her vehicle.

Pulling up to their house a little over an hour later, after stopping to get herself dinner, she saw that Kennedy's vehicle was in the driveway. "Well shoot, I hope she wasn't waiting long," she commented, looking at Rowdy who just tilted his head at her. Shutting the vehicle off and getting out, Keeley grabbed her bags and dinner, and opened the back door for Rowdy to jump down. Hearing Kennedy shut her door she turned around, only for

Rowdy to stand in front of her protectively. Smiling, she patted his head and told him, "She's family." Seeing Rowdy relax had Keeley relaxing, too.

Seeing Kennedy's shock at Rowdy had her worried, until she squealed out, "Oh my God, he's freaking adorable!!" Running over she dropped down in front of him, about a foot away and held out her hand while cooing to him. When Rowdy looked to her she nodded, knowing that even though someone had abandoned him, he was going to be ok with her. He was a very smart boy. As he closed the gap to Kennedy, she admired his body. He was snow white in color with eyes nearly the same color as hers, crystal clear blue. She had to admit that's what she liked most. He was a pretty healthy size and she hadn't noticed any skittish tendencies in him, so that made her happy that wherever he was before they took good care of him, but it also made her wonder who could possibly abandon such a sweetheart.

Kennedy interrupted her thoughts when she asked, "What's his name and where did you get him?"

Explaining how she came to find him and what the circumstances were, she started to worry that Nathaniel and Tyler wouldn't accept him. "Do you think Tyler and Nathaniel will be angry with me? I never thought to ask them. I just acted on impulse, they were going to kill him, and I couldn't let that happen." Keeley worried.

"Oh please, you have those two wrapped around your little finger. Even if they hated dogs, which they don't, they would still keep him. But seeing how protective he was when I got out, I'd say you have nothing to worry about. That alone will have him worming his way into their hearts," she said smiling and laughing at Rowdy's antics, as he roamed the yard sniffing and peeing on everything in sight, marking his territory.

Getting up and making their way to the porch swing, they watched Rowdy for a bit before Keeley asked why she was here.

"Oh, well, I knew they left and thought you might want some company. I should have called or texted first, but I was excited that we might have a girls' night. But it's getting late and we both have to work tomorrow, so maybe this weekend I'll come over with some cheesy movies and we can veg out?" Kennedy asked her hopefully.

"Yes, I would love that. I'll meet you here after work on Friday night?"

With a thumbs up, Kennedy said goodnight and made her way to her own car. Pulling out she honked her horn once and waved out the window.

Getting up, Keeley went to grab all of Rowdy's stuff from her SUV. "Come on boy, you help." She laughed holding out a bag for him, shocked when he grabbed it and trotted up the steps to the front door. She yelled, "Where'd ya learn that trick?" Locking the SUV she made her way to the steps. Unlocking the door, Rowdy bounded into the house, heading straight for the kitchen. Smiling at his cleverness, she dropped his bed and toys in the living room, before going to the kitchen and putting his dog food in the pantry. After filling his bowl with food and getting him some water, Keeley sat down at the breakfast bar with her dinner.

Cleaning up, she made her way up to their room. Missing Nathaniel and Tyler like crazy, she sent them each a quick text.

> **K:** Miss you like crazy Nathaniel, hope you landed safely. Sweet dreams. Love, your Butterfly.
>
> **K:** Missing your sweet dimples, please stay safe. Love you, Keeley.

Putting her phone down on the nightstand, she stripped and grabbed one of Tyler's t-shirts. Slipping it on, it came to mid-thigh and could easily fit two of her in it. Laying down in bed after shutting the light off, she heard Rowdy drop down onto the floor. Laughing at how he sounded like he just collapsed, she whispered, "Night Rowdy", before she fell into a fitful sleep.

Chapter 16

W HEN FRIDAY ROLLED around and Keeley still hadn't heard from the guys, other than the text they sent her to say they got there safe and they loved her, she was trying not to worry, but it was hard. Having not spoken to them since they left on Tuesday was hard for her, but at least she had Rowdy for company, so she wasn't isolated and alone when she wasn't working.

As she was about to leave for lunch, her desk phone rang. Picking it up, she was surprised by the menacing voice on the other end. "Bitch, you and those hound dogs better leave my Emily alone. She's mine and you need to back off!" He yelled the last part at her, before hanging up. Still in shock, she jumped when Dane and Coop walked by her office, laughing about something.

"You alright, kid?" Coop asked her.

Shaking her head and taking a deep breath, she prepared to tell them about the phone call. "I think Emily's stalker just called."

"WHAT!" They exploded at the same time, coming towards her. "Are you alright?" Dane asked. Nodding her head, she explained everything the man had said.

"Shit. When was the last time you spoke to Emily? I haven't heard from her since our initial meeting, Wednesday morning," Coop said.

"I talked to her yesterday and she was fine; spooked, but otherwise fine. Do you think she's ok?"

"We'll go check on her, see how she's doing. Why don't you call Kennedy and the two of you can start your girls' night early," Dane suggested. Nodding her head, she grabbed her stuff, while they went to their offices. Worried about Emily, Keeley sent her a quick text.

> **K:** Everything ok?
>
> **E:** Fine. Why, what's wrong?
>
> **K:** Nothing. Just wanted to check in. Call me if you need me. Or the guys.
>
> **E:** Thanks, I will.
>
> **K:** Hey, you should come to girls' night tonight, I'm leaving now, I can swing by and pick you up. Cheesy movies and junk food! You know you wanna ;)
>
> **E:** I don't want to intrude.
>
> **K:** You won't. I'll be there in 15! :D

Feeling better knowing Emily won't be alone, she walked to Dane and Coop's office. "Hey guys, I'm going to pick Emily up on my way home. She's coming for girls' night."

"Is that a good idea? For all we know this guy has gone off his rocker and might try something." Coop worried.

"It's fine. I have Rowdy, and we'll call if we get scared

160

or something happens.

Sighing because they knew she wouldn't give in, they both nodded their heads and told her to have fun. Saying goodbye, she sent a quick text to Kennedy telling her of the change in plans.

PULLING UP TO Emily's house, Keeley honked the horn twice and waited for her to come out. A couple minutes later, Emily was out the door and locking it. Running to Keeley's SUV with a smile on her face, she jumped in and exclaimed, "Thank you so much for this. I've never had a girls' night before. I'm really excited." Her smile and laughter was infectious, and soon they were laughing like old friends.

"Kennedy will be meeting us at my house in a couple hours," she told her, starting the drive back home. Pulling into the driveway, Keeley smiled when Rowdy jumped off the porch swing. She had tried to leave him inside every day, but he refused to go in when she left for work. He was one very stubborn dog. After that first morning, she thought she would come home to a missing dog, but as far as she knew he didn't stray too far. He always sat on the porch when she left, and was on the swing when she came home. It gave her a sense of relief knowing he was here, protecting the house, when she and the guys couldn't be.

Getting out she noticed Emily looked weary about him. Trying to comfort the other woman, she told her,

"He's a rescue. Very sweet though. I haven't even heard him bark yet. He also seems to be quite the ladies man." Smiling and laughing because he was now laying on the ground inching his way to Emily. whining, and with what she could only describe as a smile on his face. Stopping a foot away from Emily, Rowdy rolled over to his back, paws up, wanting her to rub his belly.

Relief washed through her when Emily walked closer and started to rub his belly. Laughing when he licked her hand, she looked to Keeley. "He's just a big baby, isn't he?" She cooed to him.

Shaking her head at Rowdy's antics she made her way to the door, unlocking it and walking in, leaving it open for them. Going straight to her room to change into shorts and a tank top, she marveled at how much her life had changed in the last month. She had friends, two very protective pseudo big brothers, and she was in a relationship with two of the most handsome and devoted men she'd ever met. For the first time she could remember, she was happy and free. Her self-esteem was at an all-time high. She wouldn't say she was over what happened in her life before meeting Nathaniel and Tyler, but she was confident that she would at least have a happy life, and be able to move forward.

Hearing Rowdy bounding up the stairs, she started to make her way towards him and head back down. Entering the kitchen, Emily was just sitting on a stool looking around in awe. "This is a very gorgeous kitchen, I bet you love cooking in here!"

"I will admit it's one of my favorite rooms in the house." Keeley told her, making her way to the fridge to pull out the platters she had made the previous evening, for tonight. When her phone dinged, she went back to the entryway to retrieve it from her purse. Looking at it she saw two texts from the guys. Opening the one from Nathaniel first, she smiled.

N: *Missing you like crazy, should be home Sunday. Love you <3*

K: *Looking forward to it. I have a surprise ;) Love you!*

Opening the one from Tyler she laughed out loud.

T: *Miss your sexy ass, what are you wearing? Love ya!*

K: *Miss you too, and not much! See you soon, much love <3*

Putting her phone back, she made her way to the pantry to grab Rowdy his treat. "Here you go, boy." Watching him walk away after she gave it to him, Keeley gestured to Emily to follow her out back to wait for Kennedy to get there. "How are you really doing, Em?"

Looking at her, she could see the fear and uncertainty lurking in her eyes; she knew the feeling all too well. "I don't know Keels, I'm so scared to do anything anymore. It's been so long since I've felt safe. Like I could live my life again. I just don't know what I'll do if Dane and Cooper can't find this person," she said sounding defeated.

Reaching over to her, she grabbed her hand and

squeezed it saying, "We will all do everything possible to find this person, and make sure he gets locked up for as long as possible."

Nodding her head at Keeley, she stared off, lost in thought. Shaking her head Emily looked back to her and said, "No more drama talk, tonight is about fun. I've never had a girl's night before."

Smiling at Em, she confessed, "Neither have I, but I think we're in for a real treat with Kennedy in charge." As they were laughing, Kennedy came around the side of the house asking, "What's so funny? You didn't start the party without me did you?" She cajoled with a fake pout, before bursting out laughing.

"Ok ladies, I have movies, I bought as much ice cream as I can carry, AND I brought everything needed for manicures and pedicures," Kennedy said, turning and walking back to her car. Getting up and following her, Keeley was shocked at just how much ice cream she brought.

"Geez what'd you do, buy out the whole aisle?" she asked her only half kidding.

"What? It's girls' night, your men aren't here, Emily has some psycho stalking her, and me? Well, I got nothing, I'm boring. I think we could all use some icy relief," Kennedy dead-panned, grabbing the movies and instructing her and Emily to get the rest.

After they had everything inside and most of the ice cream in the freezer, they set up their snacks, mani/pedi stuff, and movies in the living room. Leaving no surface empty with their things. Choosing to watch *Pretty in Pink* first, they set up to do Emily's nails for their impromptu spa. Keeley did her nails a bright yellow, while Kennedy did her toes a soft pink. They talked about everything and anything, so long as it wasn't heavy and heart-breaking.

Hearing Rowdy growling and scratching at the back door after they finished all of their nails, and had just popped their third movie of the evening in, *Grease*, Keeley went over to investigate what had him so worked up. "What's the matter, boy?" She asked walking into the kitchen and turning on the light. When he barked again and looked at her, she unlocked and opened the door for him to go out.

When he took off for the woods behind the house, she chased after him, calling out his name. Stopping at the edge of the tree line, she didn't go in any farther, since the sun was just setting and she knew finding her way out would be unlikely. Going back to the house, she didn't want to worry the girls but saw no way around it. "Hey guys, Rowdy's acting funny and took off for the woods when I let him out. I'm gonna call Dane, see if he can come take a look around."

Grabbing her phone, she dialed him. Answering after the first ring he barked out, "What's wrong?"

"Hello to you too, Dane. Girls' night is great, how is yours?" She asked sarcastically.

"Keeley," he growled out.

"Ok, ok, sheesh. Look, Rowdy was barking and scratching at the door and when I let him out he took off for the woods, and he's not coming when I call him. It's too dark for me to go in there. Will you come see if you can find him, please?" She asked knowing the worry she felt about her dog's odd behavior was bleeding through in her voice.

"We're on our way," was all he said, ending the conversation as abruptly as it started.

"Well, grumpy pants is on his way with Coop, I assume," she relayed to Kennedy and Emily, since they both looked slightly worried.

Looking out the big bay window in the living room, she couldn't help but be worried someone was out there. What if it was Emily's stalker? What would they do?

HEARING A VEHICLE pull up out front a little while later, all three girls raced out the front door to see Dane and Coop climbing out of their truck. "Could you have taken any longer?" Kennedy asked smartly, earning a growl from Coop.

"Watch it little girl, or I'll put you over my knee," he threatened, making her stick her tongue out at him. Chuckling, he called her a brat, before they went around back to check things out and see if they could find Rowdy.

"You girls get back inside and lock the doors until we get back," Dane shouted following Coop. Sighing, they all went back inside to wait.

A little while later when Keeley heard Rowdy's nails

clicking on the porch, she ran for the door to see the guys coming from the woods and talking quietly. "Well?" She asked impatiently.

Giving a sigh, they looked at each other before answering her. "I think it was a deer or coyote, but we're staying the night, and we'll take a closer look in the morning."

"Well there goes girls' night!" Kennedy said dramatically.

"You're pushing it, Ken!" Coop said teasing her, knowing she hated that name. Kicking his shin, she stomped back into the house. "Shit!" He exclaimed.

Laughing at their juvenile teasing, Keeley called Rowdy in and started cleaning up the living room and kitchen, before saying good night and going to bed, knowing Dane and Coop would find their own place to sleep.

The following morning after the guys checked things over in the light of day, and the girls had gone home, she started cleaning the house and getting things ready for when Nathaniel and Tyler came home on Sunday.

Hearing a car door slam outside had her slightly confused. Heading to the front door with Rowdy following close behind, she opened it and was startled when the dog started growling and baring his teeth. Looking up she saw who it was; definitely not someone she expected to see ever again.

Before she had a chance to grab Rowdy, and go back inside and shut the door, a gun was pulled out and leveled at her chest. Freezing from shock and fear, she didn't know what to do.

"You thought you could just live a happy life, after everything you've done to me you ungrateful bitch?" The person snarled at her menacingly, walking closer, only stopping when Rowdy let out a loud, ferocious bark.

Chapter 17

SHOCK AT SEEING her father again, held Keeley immobile with fear. "What are you doing here?" She asked. "You kicked me out."

"You're such an ungrateful cunt," he retorted. "You think you deserve all this, after the hell your mother and I put up with when she had you." Mack was waving his hand around, indicating her surroundings. "Do you know how many times we had to move because you just couldn't stop whining and crying about your punishments? Hell, we had to move clear across the country and change our names, when your stupid bitch of a grandmother wouldn't let shit go. Dumb old hag couldn't just fucking die." Keeley could hear the slurring of his words now.

Not wanting to say anything to anger him further, she stood there trying to come up with a plan, wishing Nathaniel and Tyler were here with her now. Or even Dane and Coop. When Rowdy started growling again, she looked at him to see his gaze fixed on the woods. Watching where he was, she felt a huge sense of relief when she recognized Nathaniel's bulky form moving along the tree line.

Knowing she had to distract her father, she slowly started walking down the steps, with Rowdy matching each one. Gaining his attention once again, she did something she never thought she would do, and yelled at her father, telling him what she thought of him and her mother. "It's your fault, you know," she antagonized. "You guys didn't have to have me. Hell, you could have given me up for adoption for all I would have cared. Anything would have been better than having the stigma of being Mack and Judy Stone's child. It was horrifying that people knew I was the product of you two. I hated my life. I wished for you to kill me, so many times. But you know what? I'm glad you didn't, because now...," pausing to take a breath she continued, "now I get to live the life I deserved, with two men who love me and show me that love daily. Knowing I'm better than you gives me such relief. And when I do have kids, because I will have a bunch, they'll never even know you exist. They'll know the love of what a REAL parent is like." Emphasizing her point she put both hands to her stomach, implying she could be pregnant now.

"You bitch! You always thought you were better than everyone, but you're no better than the scum-filled whorehouse you were conceived in. Tell me something, Keeley," he sneered her name like it was filth. "Do your men know you were born addicted to crack? Do they know you're just as worthless now as you were at birth?" He lied.

Seeing Nathaniel pause, she knew he was shocked to learn that her parents really did hate her. "What you fail to remember Mack, is that I am better than you. And you'll have to live with that for the rest of your life. I fucking hate you, but after today you will no longer be a speck on my radar. I will never think of you again," she told him and turned, knowing Tyler and Nathaniel had her back. Tensing when she heard the crack of a gun, Keeley expected to feel the burn of a bullet. Not feeling anything she turned around, only to be pulled into Tyler's arms. Squeezing her as tight as he could she finally squeaked out, "I can't breathe", before he let her go, looking her over from head to toe.

"Don't ever fucking provoke someone with a gun again, darlin'!" Tyler admonished her angrily, but she could also hear the worry in his voice, and see it in his eyes. "You understand, baby? I can't..., no, I won't, fucking lose you! Not now!" Burying his face in her neck, she held on for dear life. As the adrenaline started to leave her body, she started shaking violently. When Tyler called Nathaniel over, it sounded like he was yelling through a tunnel; her vision started to get cloudy with black dots, and she knew she was going to pass out. Accepting the blackness she let go, knowing her men would keep her safe.

"SHIT, NATE, SHE'S passing out." Ty called to his brother. Looking over his shoulder, he saw Nate shake his head in the negative with his fingers on Keeley's dad's neck. Knowing his brother so well, he knew taking her father's life was going to weigh heavily on his mind. Walking over to him with an unconscious Keeley in his arms, he told Nate, "You take her inside, I'll call this in. She's safe man. That's all that matters. Don't beat yourself up, yeah?" At Nate's nod, Ty thought he just might be ok. It really was a kill or be killed situation, only in this case it would have been Keeley dead, instead. And he knew that wasn't an option.

Calling for the police and an ambulance to make sure she was ok, Ty went into the house, pausing when he saw Nate sitting on the couch with Keeley still passed out in his lap. To his surprise there was a very gorgeous dog with its head resting on her stomach, and he was whining. Looking up when Ty walked in the room, the dog chuffed and went back to its vigil watch over their girl.

"Think this was her surprise?" Ty asked Nate who sat there watching the dog.

"Pretty sure it was. Dane sent that text about watching for snow. Didn't really get it at the time. I do now," he mused chuckling.

"He has her eyes. That's kinda weird, isn't it?" Ty wondered out loud, sitting down and grabbing her feet to put in his lap. "I wonder if what they say about pets looking like their owners is true. Maybe he liked her so much his eyes changed." Chuckling at his own joke, Ty wasn't prepared for the heel to his gut. Rubbing his stomach, he looked to Keeley and laughed. "Sorry darlin',

I was only kidding. But damn, am I glad to see those beauties open up for me."

Sitting up she said smiling, "I thought you weren't supposed to be home until tomorrow?" Rubbing her cheek on Nate's chest, Ty was incredibly glad they came home early.

"The job ended early Butterfly, and I'm fucking glad it did. How you doin'?" Nate asked cupping her cheek.

"I missed you both so much," she whispered with tears in her eyes.

When there was a knock on the door, the dog started growling viciously. "Calm, Rowdy," she whispered and put her hand on his head. He shocked them both when he immediately stopped and licked her hand, before rubbing his head against her leg and walking to the door, waiting for someone to open it so he could investigate.

Barking when no one came, Ty got up and said, "I'm coming boy, calm your eager ass down." Opening the door, Ty was relieved to see the same officer from a few weeks ago that drug the crazy viper away.

Explaining everything that went down, and not wanting to disturb Keeley too much until the paramedics arrived, they spoke outside. As the paramedics were looking her over, Nate came outside to explain his side of things and give his statement. Pulling Ty aside, he had a look of shock on his face.

"What's wrong, is Keeley ok?" Ty asked him worried she was injured.

"No, it's just they're checking her out and asking a

shit load of questions, but then they asked if she could be pregnant. I know she's been getting the birth control shot, but damn, do I ever wish…" he trailed off.

Thinking about that Ty looked at the house, then to his brother and whispered, "We'll just have to try harder." He winked and Nate burst out laughing, but nodded his head in agreement.

LYING IN BED that evening, after they'd thoroughly and slowly loved Keeley, Nate had time to reflect on what went down with her father. Looking down at her sleeping between him and Ty, Nate felt an innate sense of relief that they came home early. He kept obsessing over the fact that had they not, she would probably be dead. Having to shoot someone was never easy, but killing them always had his heart, mind, and conscience waging war on him. His heart knew he loved Keeley, his head knew he had to protect her at all costs. But his conscience knew he'd killed another human being, and it was eating away at his soul. It was not something he could just brush off. Nate knew it would take time to heal from, so he just hoped she could forgive him for his part in her father's death. The thought of losing her left him feeling panicky and overwhelmed. He needed her in their lives; she was as essential to them as breathing. There was nothing they wouldn't do for her. Killing her father wasn't an easy thing to do, but he knew it was either her father or Keeley.

The following morning Nate slipped out of bed. Shaking Ty awake he whispered, "We need to talk", before heading to the shower, knowing Ty would follow suit by getting up quietly and showering in another washroom.

Ten minutes later, Nate was in the kitchen making coffee when Ty strolled in. Not wanting to put it off he said, "I want to marry her. I want to ask her tonight."

Looking towards Ty, he had a huge smile on his face. Relief surged through Nate, knowing they were on the same page where Keeley was concerned. "Good, I'll call the dads and see if they still have Nonna's engagement ring stored for us." As Nate called their parents, Ty started making bacon and scrambled eggs, knowing she wouldn't sleep too long once they left the bed.

After a solid fifteen minutes of listening to their mother squealing about the fact that they were asking Keeley to marry them, Nate was finally able to get off the phone. As he was hanging up, she walked into the kitchen scowling and said, "You left me." Grabbing a coffee mug to fill for her, Nate handed it to her, getting a quick kiss in before she could complain much more. "Sorry Butterfly, we just didn't want to wake you up." He smiled at her. "Mom and the dads will be by early this afternoon though." Seeing her face light up over that made him happy. Happy that she loved his parents, and happy his parents loved her enough to treat her like a second daughter.

As soon as Ty placed her food in front of her, she dug

in saying, "I'm so hungry I could eat for two!", before diving back in, making him and Ty look at each other. Knowing they were thinking the same thing—Could she be pregnant? Shaking off the thought, Nate knew it was unlikely but couldn't help hoping that just maybe she was.

On pins and needles most of the morning, worried about how they were going to propose, Nate went down to the gym to burn off some energy.

After a heavy workout he went upstairs, only to see Ty in the kitchen packing what looked like a picnic. "What's this?" He asked him.

"Well, I figured we need a plan, right? And Keeley's not huge on pomp and crowds, so what better way to propose than a candlelight picnic under the stars." Ty smiled at his brilliant idea.

Clapping him on the back, Nate looked around for their shining star. Not seeing or hearing her anywhere in this house, he looked to Ty with a raised eyebrow. "Oh yes, well mom and the dads got here about twenty minutes ago and the dads have Keeley out back distracted, marveling over that damn dog. I swear, he's getting all the attention now," he grumbled. "Mom brought all this in and told me her idea."

"Ah, so the romance was not your doing then, huh? Did they bring the ring?" Nate asked eager to see it.

Pulling it from his pocket, Ty handed it to Nate saying, "They took it to get cleaned, too. I don't remember that engraving though. But Mom says it was always there." Ty said sounding suspicious.

Opening the box, Nate pulled it out and admired the intricate, yet simple design. It was an infinity symbol wrapped around a small blue sapphire. One line had diamonds along it, weaving from one side of the ring and around to the halfway mark, while the other was a smooth white gold that wrapped from one side of the sapphire down and around to where the diamonds ended on the opposite side.

Smiling at how perfect it was, knowing the sapphire was Keeley and the two different weaving lines would represent him and Ty, Showing them all as one love, one life wrapped together, Nate was pleased with it. Noticing the engraving Ty had mentioned, he took a closer look at it; it said *3 lives 1 love.* Smiling at it, Nate knew that was from their parents, but it was perfect.

Hearing her and their dads coming, he quickly put it back in the box and shoved it in his pocket. Smiling when she came right to him, giving him a small kiss on the lips. "Hi, Nathaniel," she said sweetly, before moving over to Ty and doing the same.

"Well, we're gonna head out, you kids have a good evening," their dad, Andrew, said before waving and grabbing their mom's hand while she yelled out, "Call me tomorrow, Keeley!"

"Butterfly, come with me, I've gotten something for you." Nate grabbed her hand and led her upstairs, to give her the sexy red dress and matching shoes Bella had given them that day they took her shopping, not so long ago.

FOLLOWING NATHANIEL UPSTAIRS, Keeley wondered at their odd behavior today. They kept giving each other funny looks and they seemed twitchy. Putting it to the back of her mind to ask them about later, she was excited to see what Nathaniel had for her. Stepping into his old room, she followed him to the closet where he pulled out the most beautiful red halter dress she had ever seen. "Oh Nathaniel, it's beautiful. Thank you," she effused, taking it from him and holding it to her body, knowing it was going to fit like a glove.

The top would be tight to her skin, from her breasts to her hips, where it would flare out to reach just above her knees. Looking up at Nathaniel, she saw he was smiling and holding a gorgeous pair of red peep-toe pumps that matched. "What's the occasion?" She asked.

"We just want to have a nice romantic evening, will you wear it?" He asked her with a smug smile on his face, knowing she was in love with the outfit and would wear it for them.

Nodding her head she asked, "When do I need to be ready?"

Looking at his watch he said, "You've got two hours." Kissing her forehead he walked out, leaving her to scramble to get ready. *Thank God, I showered this morning,* she thought walking back to their shared room. Knowing immediately that she wouldn't be able to wear a bra with it, she grabbed the sexiest panties she could find.

A pair of white lace boy shorts that she knew hugged her just right to showcase her ass cheeks. They had a cute little black bow on the front that sits just above her pubic line.

Setting her dress and panties on the bed, Keeley went to the bathroom to begin curling her hair in soft spiral curls. Knowing how much Nathaniel and Tyler liked to run their fingers through it, she used very little product. Happy with how it looked, she moved on to makeup. Only using some eye shadow to make her eyes smoky, and a light layer of mascara, she was done.

Looking at the time, she noticed more than an hour had passed. Stripping off her clothes she grabbed her panties, slipping them on and turning to double check in the mirror that they did in fact do wonders for her ass. Smiling, she turned to put the dress on over her head, it glided down her body, stopping when the top hit her hips. Pulling the top of it up, she tied the straps around her neck and adjusted her breasts, so nothing was popping out.

Giving a small tug brought the skirt down to rest where it was meant to. Looking in the mirror, she loved how the top molded to her curves and the bottom was light and flirty, moving with her. Sitting on the settee in the corner, she put on the matching red pumps, very glad that her and the girls did mani/pedis on Friday night, before all the chaos had begun.

Looking herself over she decided to put on a soft pink lipstick, and finding a small barrette with light pink and white flowers, she pulled the hair back behind her ear on the left side. With one last look she was done.

Walking down to the living room, she saw the guys were all ready to go. Nathaniel looked handsome in his navy blue dress pants molded to his thighs, and a white shirt, sleeves rolled to his elbows, and buttoned only half way up. He looked good enough to eat. Looking at Tyler, he was just as delicious. Wearing a pair of white dress pants and a gray button-up shirt, worn similar to Nathaniel, Keeley was ready to strip down right there.

"Wow... fuck... damn... you look good enough to eat, Butterfly," Nathaniel said sounding out of breath, making her blush. With a whispered, "Thank you", she bent her head, trying to get away from his very intense gaze. The look he was giving her was making her squirm. Squeezing her legs together to try and relieve the pressure, she was startled when Tyler came over kneeling in front of her, looking her in the eyes with a fire burning in their gorgeous hazel depths. Grabbing her hips he nuzzled her belly and told her, "You're fucking stunning darlin', never seen a better sight than you in siren red." He smirked over the last part making her giggle.

"You both look good enough to eat, too," she told them sincerely. "Where are we going?" She asked as they grabbed what looked like the picnic basket Tyler was making earlier, and walked out the back door. Smiling at her neither of them answered, leaving Keeley to wonder what their plan was but happy to go along, because they both seemed very excited about something.

Walking just past the tree line she noticed a blanket laid out with tiki torches lit at each corner. Looking at them in shock, she saw they were both smiling at her, before pulling her the rest of the way. Nathaniel helped her sit down, while Tyler pulled out their dinner from the basket. Still in awe at their thoughtful and romantic gesture, she wordlessly took the plate Tyler gave her. Looking at the variety of foods: fruit, cheese, luncheon meats, crackers, and some vegetables, she just mindlessly ate her food, while keeping a close eye on her men.

Their matching smiles left her curious as to what this was really about. When Nathaniel pulled out a bottle of champagne and filled three glasses, her heart started to beat out of control at what the possibilities could be for such a celebration. Not saying anything, she took the glass from him and waited.

Holding up their glasses she followed suit, placing hers between theirs. "A toast," Tyler suggested. "To a fresh start and a new love." He smiled clinking their glasses together and drinking. When Keeley was finished with hers Tyler grabbed it, placing it back in the basket where they put theirs. When they both kneeled beside her, Nathaniel on her right and Tyler on her left, they each grabbed one of her hands, kissed her on each cheek before Tyler began speaking. "Keeley, before you came into our lives I didn't know anything was missing, or that half my heart was empty. I thought I knew love and connection, but you have taught me so much. That to really own someone else's heart, I had to work for it harder than anything else in my life. I love you and right here, right now, I'm making you a promise to love and protect you and your love for us, with every fiber of my being." When he was done she had tears in her eyes, her heart was beating furiously, and she was at a loss for words. She could see everything he was promising her in his eyes, and she fell even more in love with him in that moment.

Feeling a squeeze in her other hand, she looked to Nathaniel. "Butterfly, when we met, it was like a punch to gut. You captivated me from the minute I saw you. There's nothing in this world I wouldn't give you. You've taught me that with love comes patience and understanding, a commitment so deep I no longer know where you end and I begin. Without you in our lives we would be happy, but we wouldn't know what true love and devotion was." Pulling something from his pocket, Nathaniel put the most gorgeous ring she had ever seen on her left ring finger and pledging, "With this ring we give you us for eternity, our love, our lives, everything we are. We love you Keeley, will you do us the honor of becoming our wife?" Speechless and with tears streaming down her face, all she could do was nod her head yes.

LETTING OUT THE breath he'd been holding since he finished talking, Nate grabbed Keeley around the back of her neck and slammed his mouth down on hers, after slipping the ring on her finger. Finally feeling like everything was falling into place with their lives, Nate felt complete, as if he had finally found his purpose in life. She was a living, breathing entity and the most beautiful sight he'd ever seen.

When she came downstairs in that tight, yet flirty dress, his heart stopped and he couldn't breathe for a full minute. The top fit her like a second skin, it held her breasts in like he was holding them. High and perky, with just enough cleavage to tantalize his senses and draw him in to her siren's call.

Pulling away from the allure of her lips, he looked deeply into the most gorgeous blue eyes he'd ever seen saying, "Thank you, Butterfly. Giving us the gift of you is the best thing we'll ever get," before kissing her again. Nibbling on her lips lightly, Nate bit down on her bottom one, making her moan from the dual sensations of pleasure and pain. Sucking it into his mouth, he felt Ty move in behind her and undo the strings to her top.

Pulling away for it to drop, Nate sat on his heels to look at her. "Your magnificent, Keeley," he told her reverently. Looking at her, she put her head down in shyness, causing some of her curls to fall forward, covering her breasts. Nate grabbed the camera from the basket and snapped a shot. With her head bent and her hair covering most of her breasts, she looked like a goddess. With the sun setting behind her it gave her an ethereal glow, casting a spotlight on her, like a beacon of light pointing the way home.

Noticing Ty's impatience at making love to her, Nate

started to undress, with his blood pumping so fast he felt like he was in a race, until he looked down to Keeley. She sat with a look of unadulterated lust and love on her face, as she watched the both of them strip. Motioning for Ty to lie down, he helped her to her feet, pulling her dress the rest of the way off as she stood. As it pooled at her feet, Nate got a good look at her nearly naked body. The white panties turned him on more than he thought possible; they represented her innocence and purity. Growling, he grabbed the little bow with his teeth and gave one sharp tug, ripping them from her body. Grabbing them up, he locked eyes with her before bringing them to his face and inhaling her womanly scent. At her blush, he bent forward and licked her sweet smelling pussy from top to bottom, before coming back up to her clit and sucking hard, making her scream out in rapture. "Music to my ears," he said smugly. "Hop up on Ty, Butterfly, and show him that golden pussy." He smirked at the shocked look she shot him.

"Oh ya, baby, show me how much you love me." Winking at her Ty grabbed her hips, pulling her to kneel above him. Swiping his hand through her slit, Ty lined up his already leaking cock and slowly pulled her down his shaft, until she was resting fully on top of him.

Pressing his chiseled chest to her smooth back, Nate told her, "Lay flat Butterfly, this sexy ass is mine tonight." Smoothing his hand down the sleek line of her back, Nate grabbed hold of her perfect ass cheeks and massaged them lightly, before pulling them apart to look at her pretty rosebud. Bending down he blew a thin line of air over her, and watched in fascination as a shiver worked its way up her spine. Kissing each pale, beautiful globe, he pulled back and reached into the basket to grab the lube.

After applying a generous amount on her asshole, he started to rub it in. Slipping one finger inside, Nate moved it around before putting another in. At her moan of pleasure, he knew they were in for the ride of a lifetime. Applying some gel to his rock hard cock, he bent down and whispered in her ear, "You ready for me to own you, Butterfly?" When she looked over her shoulder at him with bliss in her eyes and a smile on her face, he gently started to push in. Forging his way through the tight ring of muscle and her sharp intake of breath, he took a moment to let her get used to it. When she started to wiggle, he pushed forward until his pelvis met her ass cheeks.

As soon as Keeley sighed and melted into Ty, they started a smooth rhythm of Ty pulling out when Nate pushed in, until Keeley started to squeeze her walls and tried rocking back and forth on them. With Ty's hands on her hips, Nate grabbed her shoulders pulling her up and against his chest. When she moaned from the new position, pushing both of their cocks deeper into her body, Nate turned her head to kiss her plump pink lips. Nipping at her until she opened, he ran his hands under her arms and moved them up slowly, to hold her breasts, just grazing her skin with the tips of his fingers, having her shiver almost uncontrollably. Rocking into her slowly and passionately, they made love to her under the moon and stars until they were all a mess of limbs, fighting for release.

"Please Nathaniel, Tyler more, harder, faster. I just need... more." She breathed on a long, drawn-out moan. Knowing what she needed gave them great pleasure that she was lost in their passion, every bit as much as they were. With his arms still wrapped under hers, Nate moved one hand up to grab her hair and the other he gently wrapped around her throat. Feeling her juices gush from her and splash onto all of them, he knew she was in the deep throes of passion.

Seeing Ty reach for the camera, he smiled, knowing what he was doing. Nate was surprised though, when Ty lifted his other hand to wrap around her throat, at the base of her neck right under his. At her gasp, they started to pound into her furiously, while simultaneously squeezing her just a little bit. Making it so she felt her pleasure more intensely, so she was aware of every erogenous point throughout her entire body. Nate relished in the trust she gave them, knowing she wouldn't allow them to do it unless she loved and trusted them completely. When she raised her hands up to put one of each on their wrists, she squeezed them right before her body let loose in what he could only describe as complete surrender to their control. Eyes closed and mouth open on a silent scream, her body locked just as Ty snapped a picture of her in the midst of her orgasm. When she tightened her ass, Nate went off like a rocket. Throwing his head back and growling out, "Keeellleeeyyy", he came harder than he ever had before. Toes curling and muscles on lock down, Nate shot jets of cum into her ass, before finally relaxing and rubbing his hands up and down her oversensitive body.

Watching Ty grab her hips and start pounding up into her furiously, Nate whispered in her ear, "Tighten that sweet pussy on him, Butterfly." Smirking at the shock in Ty's eyes when she did, Ty came on a growl, slamming up into her one last time before letting go.

Pulling slowly from her ass, Nate rolled them to the side. Running their hands up and down her body Nate asked, "Are you happy, Butterfly?"

Looking over her shoulder at him she sighed out, "Oh Nathaniel, more than you'll ever know. I never thought I'd get my own happy ending." Closing her eyes she kissed him softly, before turning to Ty and doing the same.

Epilogue

Three months later.

WAKING UP SLOWLY from a deep sleep, after having the most marvelous dream about their wedding day; marrying Nathaniel officially at the courthouse, and then a few days later having a private ceremony for the three of them to pledge their love for each other. She felt a sense of relief in knowing she was theirs, and they were hers. Keeley got up to an empty bed and quiet house, except for Rowdy, snoring loudly on his bed in the corner. Knowing the guys had to go into work today after such a long honeymoon, she felt at peace in her new life. Knowing everything bad that happened led to her having such wonderful and attentive men, a new family she adored, and friends she loved. Keeley felt like her life was complete; except for one thing. The one thing Nathaniel and Tyler had been hinting at, and she always shied away from.

A baby.

What they didn't know though was that she wanted to surprise them with a pregnancy, knowing they would be happy no matter what. After the sexcapades of their honeymoon, and every moment before, she felt pretty confident that she probably was, since she never got her birth control shot updated two months ago.

Getting up and going to the washroom, she grabbed one of the tests she'd covertly gotten on her last trip to the drug store. Opening the package and sitting on the toilet, she peed on the stick as instructed. Setting it on the counter, she washed her hands and brushed her teeth, while waiting. Thinking about the events that unfolded before they got engaged, she knew she should have been sad or mad, or something. But what she felt was nothing. Her father had never been a real father to her, he didn't love her and he took every opportunity to tell her that. When Nathaniel had asked her for forgiveness for having to killing him she had cried, not because he was dead, but because Nathaniel felt she would be angry at him for having done it.

They had helped her give her father a proper burial, but that was all she had left for the man who hurt her for the entirety of her life. She had vowed then and there, at his grave site, not to give him anymore of herself. Shaking off the depressing thoughts, Keeley felt a kernel of excitement at what she was doing in the present.

Closing her eyes and taking a deep breath she looked at the stick. With tears in her eyes and a full heart at seeing the twin pink lines, she squealed and jumped around in her excitement. Picking up the stick and going to her nightstand to grab her cell phone, she laid down on her back on the bed, pulled up her shirt and placed the pregnancy test on her stomach. She then took a photo, sending it in a dual message to Nathaniel and Tyler. It didn't take long for her to get a response.

N: *Fuck yeah! On our way Butterfly, love you so much! <3*

T: *For real? On our way, prepare to be loved! <3*

With her heart full of love and her husbands happy, Keeley relished in the feeling of contentment, knowing she was finally where she was supposed to be.

 The End

About the Author

Krystal is a stay at home mom of 4 children who was first an avid reader, then an enthusiastic blogger, and has now finally had her dreams come true and become a writer. More often than not she can be found at home with her family, reading, writing, or scrapbooking. She is coffee addict, book-aholic, and loves to hear from her fans. Some of her favorite authors include Sapphire Knight, Jordan Marie, Honey Palomino, Leslie Wilder, Autumn Jones Lake, Joanna Blake, Cora Brent, Jenika Snow CM Steele, Kaylee Song and Maya Banks to name just a few. She loves everything book and coffee related and loves finding new authors and recommending her favorites.

You can find me on:

Facebook:

www.facebook.com/KLDonnAuthor

Twitter:

@Author_KLDonn

Blog:

kldonnauthor.blogspot.ca

Goodreads:

www.goodreads.com/author/show/14100370.K_L_Donn

Google +:

plus.google.com/u/0/107452305951652674091/posts

Please feel free to also join my street team KL's Fighters

www.facebook.com/groups/125713731097925/

Play List

These songs helped me get through some very tricky and frustrating scene's so don't laugh! Lol

The Climb by Miley Cyrus

Jungle by X Ambassador

Bad Blood by Taylor Swift

Bang Bang by Jessie J, Ariana Grande, & Micki Minaj

Something In The Water by Carrie Underwood

Little Red Wagon by Miranda Lambert

Firework by Katy Perry

This Is How We Roll by Florida Georgia Line

Guts Over Fear by Eminem and Sia

Pretty Girls by Britney Spears and Iggy Azalea

Fighter by Christina Aguilera

Made in the USA
Charleston, SC
24 November 2015